# FOREVER DIVORCED FROM ETERNITY

# EMOTIONAL ENTANGLEMENT

## FOREVER DIVORCED FROM ETERNITY
### novella one in a trilogy

## CYNTHIA EPHRON-JEFFRESS

Herself Publishing

TO GOD ALMIGHTY, who breathes on every word written with the stroke of my pen, and without him, nothing is possible.

# AUTHORS' NOTE

The Emotional Entanglement trilogy is set in Jacksonville, Florida. Some of the landmarks, such as Jacksonville International Airport, are accurately placed in their proper settings. Other buildings, parks, and establishments will be nothing more than figments of our imaginations. I hope those of you familiar with Jacksonville and the surrounding area will have fun distinguishing between the two. Emotional Entanglement is an Inspirational Romance Drama Fiction trilogy, written for readers to have a moviegoer's experience, taking a front-row seat in the theater and buckling up for a journey through friendships, relationships, and situationships, savoring the flavor of second chances.

# Chapter 1

Online dating was her final boarding call, a last-ditch flight into the unknown, and Latoya Marino clutched her metaphorical passport with a blend of excitement and trepidation. At the Jacksonville International airport, the engine roars as the large airliner glides toward Gate B4, its wheels rhythmically clicking against the tarmac. Inside the cockpit, the Captain, a clean-shaven man in his forties, grips the control yoke with unwavering focus, and the weight of the flight ahead is heavy upon him.

As the plane settles into place, a rainstorm lashes against the airport's glass windows, creating a chaotic symphony of sound in the bustling terminal. Travelers rush through busy check-in lines. The air buzzed with energy. Above, red, white, and blue decorations hang.

Crying children clutch small American flags as they weave through the crowds. Rows of customer service airline workers line the Herself Airlines' ticket counter.

"Flight 36 to Atlanta is now boarding," crackles the announcement over the loudspeaker, cutting through the air, the flight Latoya Marino was trying to catch. At Gate B4, the atmosphere buzzes with activity. Inside the airplane cabin, passengers settle into their seats, their impatience crackling in the air. A flight attendant, bright-eyed in her airline uniform, flits about, ensuring everyone finds their place and stows their luggage quickly. With a final glance over her shoulder, she closes the airplane door, a soft thud echoing through the cabin.

In the cockpit, the Captain's attention narrows to the illuminated instrument panel before him. Numerous displays and gauges indicate critical information, including altitude, speed, and navigation data. Clearing his throat, he addresses ground control with a steady voice.

"Okay, ground control, Flight 36, we're set for takeoff. Request clearance." The response crackles through the intercom.

"Flight 36, you are cleared for takeoff."

The engines roar to life as the plane accelerates down the runway, slicing through the storm. Rain batters the windshield, and lightning flashes ominously in the distance as they hurtle down the tarmac—the air shimmers with tension.

"Air speed alive – 80 knots – V1 – Rotate," the copilot announces, his voice underlined with concentration. The captain tightens his grip as he initiates the rotation. With a surge of power, the aircraft ascends, rattling against the gusts outside.

The voice of the copilot fills the cockpit once more.

"Positive rate—Gear up," he commands.

"Flaps," comes the swift reply.

"Flaps up," Captain Phillips responds, his gaze fixed on the still-fleeing ground below as they climb higher, the airport shrinking in the distance.

Meanwhile, inside the airport at the airline ticket counter stands Carmen Perez, an airline employee dressed in a freshly pressed uniform. Her ruby-red lips complement eye shadow that matches her blush, and her hair is neatly pulled away from her face. She stands tall and ready, surrounded by busy travelers, exuding a genuine passion for helping others.

"Good morning! Next passenger in line, please!" she calls out, her bright voice slicing through the drone of conversation.

Beside her stands Denise Morgan, a beautiful, curly redhead, lost in paperwork, mutters.

"I can't believe it's this busy! We haven't seen weather this bad in months!" She glances at the long queue, noticing the impatience and concern etched on each traveler's face.

Outside the terminal, an Uber pulled up to the entrance. Latoya, an off-duty airline employee in her late twenties, flung open the door and thrust her umbrella out to shield herself from the rain. Grabbing her heavy luggage, she slips, narrowly catching herself on the edge of the car before dashing through the sliding doors, leaving her umbrella behind.

Inside the terminal, Latoya's heart races as she fights through the crowd, her eyes scanning for the airline ticket counter. With one roller bag in tow and the other slung over her shoulder, she bypasses the long line and approaches Denise, her coworker, with fear and urgency etched in her features.

"Ciao!" Shouts Latoya. "Please, please tell me I haven't missed my flight to Atlanta!" Latoya gasps, her voice tinged with desperation. Denise hurriedly searches the screen for the departing flights, her face turning apologetic.

"Your flight has departed," she says gently.

Latoya's shoulders slumped, and she felt a gnawing pit form in her stomach because she wasn't going to Atlanta for work. She has plans for an important date with someone she has been looking forward to for weeks. As she turns away, conflicting emotions churn within her.

"Wait, there's another flight leaving in two hours," Denise shouts. Latoya exhales deeply, a wave of frustration washing over her.

"I can't believe I missed my flight. My Uber driver stopped for gas!" explains Latoya. Denise shakes her head sympathetically and issues a new boarding pass.

"Here's your new boarding pass. Now you have time for a bite to eat if you hurry." A glimmer of hope sparks in Latoya's eyes.

"Thanks, Denise! I really appreciate it. I could use a snack to calm my nerves."

"I'll join you—if you don't mind."

Turning off her computer, she secured the cash drawer and grabbed one of Latoya's travel bags, walking alongside her toward the food court. They entered the vibrant food court filled with a cacophony of culinary options, seating choices, and the hum of conversation. Latoya allowed herself a small smile. It seemed there might yet be a chance to salvage her day.

"May I take your orders?" a young waiter asked as they approached a bustling food counter. Latoya contemplated the choices for a moment, then ordered.

"I'll have the tuna salad."

Denise ordered a double cheeseburger, large fries, and a large Coke, a choice that drew playful scrutiny from her friend Latoya. As Latoya reached over and placed her hand on Denise's stomach, Denise quickly pushed it away, a flicker of annoyance crossing her face.

"Are you eating for two?" Latoya teased, a mischievous glint in her eyes. Denise shot her with a confused look.

"No... why would you ask me that?" Latoya pointed at the meal in front of her.

"A double cheeseburger, large fries, and a large

Coke, and it's only 7 in the morning."  "I know it's not normal," Denise replied, sighing, "but I started work at 4 in the morning."  The announcement system crackles to life, echoing through the terminal.

"All Atlanta departing flights are canceled for the day."

An immediate wave of panic washed over the waiting passengers, who rushed to the airline counters, desperation etched on their faces. The staff scrambled to assist them as lightning lit up the heavy clouds outside, heightening the tension in the air.

Latoya froze. That news felt like a body blow, and her expression shifted from playful to worried.

"I need to get to Atlanta today!" Panic rose in her voice. Her heart raced at the thought of not flying to the man she was to meet. They spark chemistry through countless messages. Now, they plan to connect in person.

"No, my flight can't be canceled — I need to get to Atlanta. This can't be happening."

"Eat up," Denise urged. "Carmen needs my help rebooking our passengers."

"I just lost my appetite—Please, you go ahead," Latoya responded, her voice strained. "I just need a minute." Latoya fished her cell phone out, anxiously dialing for answers.

At the same time, Denise dashed to the ticket counter, determination set in her stride as she began assisting passengers with their check-ins.

The scene quickly unfolded, revealing a long line of disgruntled travelers extending outside the terminal at the Jacksonville airport.

Carmen, the seasoned employee, was frantically rebooking customers, while Denise logged into her computer. Latoya, in a moment of solidarity, grabbed her luggage and headed to the back office, then returned to help.

"How can I help?" Latoya asked, her voice imbued with a desire to contribute. Carmen and Denise spoke simultaneously, their exasperation amusingly aligned.

"We wish — but you are off duty."

Voices erupted from the crowd, a cacophony of frustration.

"I am not flying to Atlanta!

"Me neither!" shouts another passenger in line. "I don't want to miss my flight! Can we get an agent to help us?" Carmen raised her hand, trying to project calm amid the chaos.

"I can take the next passenger who is not traveling to Atlanta." A voice rang out from the crowd, relaying gratitude to Carmen.

"Thank you! This is why I fly your airline. You provide excellent customer service." Though the atmosphere was charged, Denise worked quickly to rebook the Atlanta passengers, her fingers flying over the keyboard with precision.

Latoya ignored Carmen's and Denise's advice and was busy tagging the customers' checked bags, eager to make the process smoother for those in distress.

Carmen eyed Latoya sternly, "What are you doing? You are off duty. Thank you, but no thank you."

Latoya shrugged, a hint of disappointment in her expression.

"I was trying to lend a hand, but I totally understand. Can I switch my flight to tomorrow?"

Carmen nodded. "Sure, then come from behind the counter."

Latoya moved slowly from the ticket counter, her shoulders slightly slumped.

"I have a favor — I need a place to stay tonight." Carmen's warm smile returned.

"You're welcome to stay at my home. I'm only working a part-time shift today. I'll be off shortly

— then we can go."

Denise's voice cut through the air, dripping with sarcasm.

"You are more than welcome to stay at my house — just saying." Latoya chuckled lightly, shaking her head.

"Thanks, Denise. Maybe next time I'm stranded at the airport."

As the shift wound down, Denise and Carmen turned off their computers and carefully locked the money drawer. Latoya waited eagerly by the employee exit door. In the dim light of the parking lot, Latoya pulled her travel bag out and glanced at her phone before shoving it into her purse.

Carmen tossed Latoya's bag into the backseat of her sleek black BMW and settled into the driver's seat. Carmen wove skillfully through traffic.

Latoya, digging into her purse, pulled out a grilled cheese sandwich and took a bite, savoring it. Carmen glanced over, a teasing smile on her lips.

"I have food at the house if you need more to eat." Latoya licked her fingers, satisfaction evident in her eyes.

"No, it's just that I didn't get to eat anything today with all the excitement at work." Carmen's gaze flitted to Latoya's fingers, visualizing them as French fries.

"I am so hungry that I want to lick your fingers, too." With a laugh, Latoya offered the sandwich toward Carmen, but she shook her head.

"No thanks, I can wait until I get to the house. Thanks anyway."

"Who is this beautiful baby boy in the picture?" Latoya asked, pointing to a small photo hanging from Carmen's rearview mirror. Carmen's expression softened, and her fingers brushed against the picture.

"Oh, it's just a glimpse of my imagination depicting what my baby boy would look like if I decided to have a child."

Carmen drove up to her house, the exterior showing off its cozy charm. Arriving in front of a red brick garage, Carmen parked the car. Latoya leaned forward in her seat, watching keenly as they both exited the vehicle.

Latoya grabbed her bags, and they walked to the front porch before entering the welcoming home.

Carmen gestured around her, a sense of pride evident in her voice.

"Welcome to my home. Feel free to make yourself comfortable."

Latoya admired her surroundings. The kitchen featured pristine white cabinets and sleek stainless-steel appliances, with pendant lights casting a soft glow over the island. Carmen paced across the shiny tile floor while Latoya slumped at the dining table, feeling exhaustion catching up with her. Her body ached with fatigue, and every movement felt like a struggle.

"You have a beautiful home. I really love the pictures of your family hanging on the walls."

"Thank you! You know, family means everything to me," warmth radiating from her words.

Latoya nodded in understanding. "I totally get that. Family really does shape who we are. You know, my parents, both born in Italy, have been married for thirty-six years, and they're still head over heels for each other. It's a beautiful thing," beaming with pride.

"Wow! Thirty-six years, that's important. Do you have siblings?"

"No. I'm figlia unica."

"So am I. So, Latoya, what's the deal with the guy you're seeing in Atlanta? Who is he? Where did you meet him?"

Latoya picked a juicy red apple from the fruit basket and took a bite, her expression evasive as she chewed. "Passengers lash out quickly when their travel plans unravel." "You don't have to tell me."

"Carmen, do you remember that morning, I was in the baggage claim office when Ms. Jenkins, a passenger, came to see me. Her luggage didn't make the flight, so she needed to file a claim."

"Yes. I remember that you felt scared!"

"I was more than scared; she lunged at me when I said she had checked her bags in late. It got worse when I told her that the late bags couldn't be delivered and that she would have to pick them up at the baggage claim office once they arrived. She hit me with her purse! screaming, 'Yes, you will deliver my bags!'" Latoya jokes.

"I'll never forget that day. You were so scared of Ms. Jenkins that you ran out of the office shouting on the radio, 'I need a supervisor at once!' Carmen chuckles.

"Sure, I remember other times, but that one stands out for me."

"Latoya, since you're not going to answer my question, come over here, this is your room, and over here is the bathroom you have all to yourself. I am going to take a shower and then watch a movie.

"Sounds good." Carmen, where are the bath towels? I have my special soap, but I need a towel."

"Look in your bathroom; there is a closet; you can find towels there.

"I see them, they smell of fresh linen, thanks again."

"You are very welcome."

"Tell me something, Latoya, why did you divorce Max? Because looking at your pictures, you two looked so happy."

Latoya's voice shook a little as she spoke, a wave of sadness washing over her.

"You know, three years ago, not long after Max started flying as a pilot, everything just fell apart for me. I can still picture that Christmas Eve night, as if it were yesterday, when the cold air matched the chill in my heart as he told me he didn't want kids. It was one of those moments that changed everything."

Carmen, lost in her own thoughts, felt her own past surfacing. The memory of the child she had that was given up for adoption hit her harder than she expected. It was a pain she thought she had pushed away, but apparently, it was still sitting there, just below the surface. Her eyes glistened with tears.

"So, let me get this straight. You want kids, but you don't want a husband?"

"Yeah," Latoya replied, her voice barely above a whisper. "After all the betrayals and the heartbreak of realizing I wouldn't get the life I dreamed of, I felt so empty. Max's cheating echoed through our marriage like a wound that wouldn't heal, and eventually, it tore us apart. I had to let go, even though it pretty much crushed me."

"I can't even imagine how hard that must have been for you," Carmen said softly, placing a comforting hand on Latoya's shoulder. "You deserve so much more. Let's take a moment to breathe and rest tonight. Tomorrow is a new day, and we'll face whatever comes together.

* * *

The morning sun streamed through the kitchen window of Carmen's house, casting a warm glow that spilled across the breakfast table. Carmen moved with practiced ease, setting plates and pouring orange juice, as the aromas of breakfast filled the air.

In the adjacent room, Latoya stirred awake, shaking off the remnants of sleep. She quickly dressed, packed her bags, and made her way to the kitchen, where she joined Carmen at the table.

"Good morning! How did you sleep?" Latoya took a hearty bite of bacon, her eyes lighting up.

"I slept like a baby. And this breakfast is on point." Carmen nodded, relieved at Latoya's upbeat demeanor. "Good. We need to leave earlier than planned because there's an accident on I-95, causing heavy traffic delays. We want to avoid what happened yesterday."

Latoya, always ready for action, finished her meal quickly. "I'm ready to go when you are. I've already packed."

Carmen finished her coffee and moved the dishes to the sink, her thoughts shifting to the road ahead.

Latoya, still consumed by her hunger, gobbled down the last strip of bacon and chased it with the orange juice before they swiftly grabbed the bags and headed out.

Carmen slid into the driver's seat of her sleek black BMW, while Latoya opened the back door and stowed her luggage. Once they were both settled, Carmen accelerated down the street, the day's plans still fresh in their minds.

"About last night," Carmen began, her tone serious as the rain started to fall, heavy droplets bouncing off the car's roof. "I wasn't prying. I'm genuinely worried about you. I don't want anything to happen."

Latoya looked out the window, her confidence unwavering. "I know, and I appreciate your concern, but I'm a big girl. I know what I'm doing." Abruptly, the rain poured down in torrents, making it difficult for Carmen to see the road. As they navigated the slick streets, Latoya quickly buckled her seatbelt when the car skidded unexpectedly off the road.

"Jesus! Are you alright?" Carmen shouted, a mix of fear and adrenaline coursing through her. Latoya gasped, her heart racing.

"Yes! I think so. Oh my God! What just happened?"

"I'm not sure," Carmen replied, trying to regain control. "It's hard for me to see. But I'm okay. I need to take my time and drive safely."

The tension in the car hung like heavy fog as Carmen gripped the steering wheel tightly, carefully reversing and navigating back onto the road. After much stress and frustration, they finally arrived at the airport.

Carmen drove into the employee parking lot, her hands still shaking slightly as she rushed out of the car.

Latoya sat to take a breather. Her urgency did not match her friend's. As Carmen approached the terminal, Denise, Carmen's colleague, spotted her and rushed forward, pulling Carmen into a warm hug.

"It's good to see you decided to come to work. Where's Latoya?"

"She's parking the car." She took a deep breath to steady herself. "I apologize for being late; there were multiple accidents on the road, and the rain was so heavy I could barely see. I ended up running off the road."

Denise's face turned serious. "I'm relieved you both are alright. Now go quickly, check in, and help me assist our passengers."

All at once, Latoya sprinted to the ticket counter, where Denise handed her a boarding pass.

In a rush, Latoya dropped the car keys in Denise's hand before dashing towards the security checkpoint.

"Don't go getting yourself into trouble," Denise called out, a playful glint in her eye. "After all, no one wants to have a mini-me popping up on a first date! Save the parenting for when you're at least five awkward dates in!"

Latoya paused, only long enough to throw a teasing glare back at her colleague.

"Denise—why would you say that?... Don't answer. Just tell Carmen I will call her once my flight lands in Atlanta."

Carmen approached the ticket counter and quickly logged into her computer, her mind still racing. "Denise, you should be ashamed of yourself for saying that to Latoya." Denise shrugged, a mischievous smile creeping onto her face.

"You know it's the truth."

"No, it's not true! Your life is the emotional entanglement."

Later on that day, while taking a break in the food court, Denise noticed Maximus (Max) Jones, a clean-shaven, slender pilot for Aruba Airways, standing across the way. Her eyes widened with curiosity.

"Isn't that Max Jones. I wonder what's going on in his life," she mused aloud.

Carmen raised eyebrows. "Uhm, you mean Latoya's ex-husband? I don't know, and I don't care. What I do know that I'm hungry. I'm going to order lunch." "Okay, order me a large double cheeseburger with all the trimmings, an extra-large fry, and a large Coke," her focus shifting to Max. "I'm going over to say hi."

"My goodness, Denise, you order enough food to feed everyone at the airport." Carmen laughed, watching as Denise waved to Max and crossed the food court.

"Hello, Max!" Denise chirped as she reached him. Max went motionless for a moment; uncertainty etched across his face before he extended his hand. "I'm sorry, but do I know you?" Denise smiled as she shook his hand.

"No, I'm Denise. I'm a friend and coworker of Latoya."

"It's nice to meet you, Denise. How is Latoya?" he asked, his expression softening slightly as he spoke her name.

"Latoya's great! You just missed her; she flew out to Atlanta," Denise replied, sensing an underlying tension in the conversation.

"You did say your name is Denise. Listen, I need help with something. I recently moved back to Florida, and I'm hoping for a second chance with Latoya," Max admitted, his tone earnest and hopeful.

Denise's eyes widened in surprise.

"Oh wow! A second chance with Latoya—Please let me know if I can help you. Here, take my phone and put your number in it."

As Max input his number into Denise's phone, an announcement blared over the airport's intercom, cutting through the chatter.

"All remaining flights for the remainder of the day have been canceled due to the weather. Please see your respective airlines for rebooking." Denise felt her heart sink.

"Oh no… I gotta go; duty calls." She began to turn back toward Carmen, catching Max's eye once more.

"Denise, I deeply appreciate what you are doing to help me. Let's keep this confidential," Max said earnestly.

"Sure thing," she replied, tucking her phone away. With a quick wave, she rushed toward Carmen, while Max hurried out of the airport, leaving a whirlwind of emotions lingering in the air. Back at the ticket counter, Denise and Carmen worked nonstop to clear the line of passengers.

"Denise, tell me what you think about this? You know Latoya stayed over at my place last night, and we had a great chat about her personal life. She told me that she was flying to Atlanta to meet a friend that she met on some online dating site—"

"—An online dating site?"

"That's not the problem, but I would appreciate your opinion on the idea of having a baby with a total stranger in secret. I mean, the poor guy will have no idea that he is being used in that manner?"

"Wait a minute, let me get this straight, Latoya is meeting men online, going on dates, to what? Get pregnant and not tell the guy about it?"

"Uhm, I am afraid so. I shared my feelings with her. I said I wouldn't do it. But she explained her reasons. She believes it's the best choice for her."

"My *Lord*, it's prayer time!" Denise exclaimed, her voice rising with urgency and faith.

Carmen looked troubled, her brow furrowed with concern.

"Latoya is in Atlanta, as we speak, on a date with a 'friend' she has never met in person. If something were to happen, I wouldn't have a name, a description, or even a glimpse of who this person is.

I'm just going to pray for her safety."

Denise stepped closer, placing a reassuring hand on Carmen's shoulder.

"That's all we can do, my friend. However, remember that prayer is a powerful tool. It transcends fear and doubt, wrapping us in the comforting embrace of hope. We must trust that God is watching over her, guiding her steps, and surrounding her with His divine protection."

Carmen nodded, her heart warmed by Denise's steady confidence.

"You're right. In moments like these, we must lean into our faith. It's in the unknown that we often find our greatest strength, and it's where we can feel God's presence most profoundly. Let's lift her in prayer.

"Absolutely," Denise agreed, closing her eyes as they both settled into a moment of quiet reflection. "Together, let's send our love and light into the universe, believing that Latoya is safe and that a higher power is guiding her. We stand in solidarity, embracing the trust that whatever happens, she is never truly alone.

# Chapter 2

The next morning, Denise paced the break room, her brow furrowed with concern. She turned to Carmen, her voice brimming with conviction.
"I believe Max has changed. He is not the same person. He is not going to hurt her again." Carmen, arms crossed, shot her a sharp glance.

"No, Denise, you don't get to make that decision."

Both women stood, the weight of their debate lingering in the air, before they returned to the ticket counter to check in passengers. A sense of urgency filled the room as the hustle of the airport continued around them.

"Please, Carmen," Denise pressed, her tone softening. "Give Max a second chance to win Latoya's heart."

"Absolutely not. I beg you, Denise, stop this matchmaking escapade you're orchestrating," exasperation leaking into her words. They continued to attend to passengers, and the announcement of Latoya's flight arrival shifted the atmosphere in the breakroom.

"I know I shouldn't be complaining, but I am not feeling this today. I didn't sleep well last night. I tossed and turned all night, and there was no one in the bed with me. Does anyone hear me? I am crying out for help here!"

"Yes, we hear you, but we don't have time for one of your pity parties. In case you haven't noticed, the line is out the door. Get to work, please!" "Where is the love?" Denise whispers.

"The love is in that long line in front of you." Carmen smiles. "By the way, I heard from

Latoya."

"Did you say anything to her about Max?"

"No, I did not. Why would I?"

"Good, because I have an impressive plan to reintroduce Latoya to Max, that is sure to make a love connection."

"As I told you yesterday, Denise, I don't want any part of your so-called impressive plan."

"I don't need your help, because I specialize in entanglements," chuckles Denise.

"Entanglements?" Whatever, Denise.

* * *

Latoya stepped off the plane with a huge smile, excitement bubbling up inside her. "I'm back, guys!" she shouted, practically skipping to the ticket counter. Denise, waiting eagerly, lit up and waved.

"Did you bring me something?"

Latoya dove into her bag, her eyes sparkling, and pulled out a juicy Georgia peach. Denise laughed, her face glowing with delight.

"You know just how to spoil me!" She happily tucked the peach away. Carmen, standing nearby, couldn't help but smile, her eyes warm with fondness.

"Who has this week's work schedule? I need to know what time I start work tomorrow?"

"You're off until Wednesday at 5 a.m.," Denise shouts.

"Thanks, Denise. Can you make me a copy of the schedule?"

"Sure thing, by the way, Latoya—are you pregnant?"

"Uh, no! What makes you think that?" Latoya shoots back, rolling her eyes.

"She's just teasing! You know Denise is a little unhinged. Denise, we've got passengers waiting. You think you can pull it together and check them in?" Carmen asks, trying to keep the chaos under control.

"Absolutely! Next passenger, please," Denise calls out, barely stifling her laughter.

"So, Latoya, spill the tea—how'd it go?" Carmen leans in, her eyes gleaming with mischief.

"It was a complete disaster—a mechanical malfunction of epic proportions." Latoya's voice drips with sarcasm.

"A mechanical malfunction? What fresh hell happened this time?" Carmen leans in, eager for the scoop.

"Okay, you're not going to believe this. I landed in Atlanta, headed straight to baggage claim, and as I'm yanking my bags off the carousel, this pink two-seat bicycle rolls up behind me—"

"—Wait," Denise cuts in, eyes popping. "A pink two-seat bicycle? I need to hear that again."

She steps closer to Latoya, buoyed by the thrill of the outrageous.

"Yup, a full-on pink two-seat bicycle! And guess who the jokester was riding it? My date," Latoya throws her hands up, clearly in disbelief.

"So this dude rolls up on a bicycle to pick you up for your date on a bicycle? What's next, a clown car? Seriously, talk about commitment issues!" Denise bursts out laughing.

"Right? It felt like I stepped into the Wizard of Oz. I honestly expected him to break into song about rainbows," Latoya rolls her eyes. "Well, at least it wasn't a unicycle!"

"—Denise, do you have any shame? Carmen whispers, trying to keep a straight face. "Show some empathy for Latoya! Continue with the story."

"It's fine, Carmen. I was just as stunned. Daniel, that's his name, smiles at me and says, 'I'm so happy to meet you finally, Latoya.' In that moment, I became motionless—I literally froze—like a deer in headlights. Then he jumps off the bike, grabs my roller bag from the carousel, and tries to cram it into the front basket like he's in some crazy circus act."

"—Heavens above!" Denise gasped, then burst out laughing. "Just like that wicked witch of the west snatching Toto away! Please, Aunt Em, don't let him take Toto! This is too much; I'm about to pee my pants! I might as well head down the yellow brick road to the bathroom—"

"Denise, just go! Seriously, go!" Carmen urges, trying not to crack up. "Latoya, don't say anything else—head home, and I'll swing by as soon as I'm done with work. Love you, girl."

"Carmen, it honestly was the most embarrassing thing ever! He says he doesn't own a car because he lost his license over unpaid child support. Seriously? Could he not have mentioned that during our phone call? Talk about a massive red flag!" Latoya groans, facepalming.

"I feel your pain," Carmen sighs, shaking her head. "You never really know who someone is until you are face-to-face with them. But hey, you're home safe, and that's what matters. Plus, now you have an adorable story to tell at parties."

Latoya chuckles, feeling a little better. Carmen pulls her in for a hug, and as Latoya turns to leave, Denise comes back from the ticket counter, grinning.

"Is Latoya alright? Or has she joined the circus now?" Denise giggles, clearly entertained by the fiasco.

"Denise, honey, you need to pray for yourself, you're a hot mess!" Carmen quips, trying not to cackle.

"Okay, okay! I get it! But listen, God's got a message for Latoya—it's loud and clear: dating total strangers is like playing dodgeball blindfolded. You don't know when the ball's gonna hit you! This was a warning." Denise turns, still chuckling, and heads back to her post, leaving Carmen in stitches.

"Did you bring lunch today?" Carmen turns and asks Denise.

"No, what about you?

"Nope."

"I'm hungry, and it is my lunch break."

"I am hungry too. Are you going to order out, or eat the famous airport food?"

"Ordering out— I'm thinking Chinese food?"

"Yes, I was just thinking the same thing. I will place the order. What will it be for you?"

"The house fried rice, baby back ribs, and a side of steamed broccoli, size small."

"Are you pregnant?"

"Don't start, Denise."

"I'm just teasing you—anything else, nothing to drink?

"I have drinks, just the food, and hurry, go place the order."

*How did I let myself get this way? Is my life a mirror image of Latoya's life? What am I going to do?* Thoughts of Denise.

"Denise, earth to Denise, did you place the food order?"

"I did, yes, I placed the order, the food order will be ready in ten minutes."

"What did you order for yourself?"

"The same, and before you ask, no, I am not pregnant!" "Okay, I didn't say you were."

"Carmen— have I told you lately how much I treasure our friendship?"

"I don't have any money to loan you!" Carmen smiles.

"You're funny. I don't need any money. I am serious, I want you to know that I treasure our friendship."

"I love you too, Denise. "Now, can we eat our lunch?"

"This house fried rice is kicking, and these ribs are scrumptious," Denise said as she licks her fingers.

"Denise, I can't help but notice how much food you order; it's enough to feed an entire Little League soccer team! Are you going to eat both shrimp egg rolls? If not, could I have one? "Here, I can't eat two."   "Thanks. Uhm, uhm, delicious!" moans Carmen.

"I agree," Denise replied.

"Slow down, Denise, you're eating like a hungry hostage. No one is going to take your food. I tell you, if I did not

know any better, I really would think you were eating for two," Carmen giggles.

"It's not that, I just love Chinese food, it's my favorite."

"Also, a double cheeseburger, extra cheese with a large fry, if my memory serves me correctly," said Carmen.

"That's right."

"Eat up. Our break is almost over; it's time to get back to our passengers."

"Tell me something, why is the check-in line just as long as it was this morning? Where is everyone going?"

"Let's see, work, school, job interviews, vacations, just to name a few places."

"I am not complaining, it is just that I am on four hours of overtime, which emakes for a long day, and it never fails when you're on overtime, all the flights are booked full, no easy money today," Carmen sighs.

"Look at the bright side: you are off tomorrow; you can sleep in late and plan how to spend all that money you made today."

"Wow! Encouragement. Thanks, Denise.

The supervisor walked up to the counter, her fingers drumming anxiously on the ticket counter as she scanned the frustrated crowd. Her brow wrinkled, and she glanced at her watch, shifting her weight nervously.

"I have two overtime shifts for tomorrow morning, 8 a.m. until 12 noon; any takers?" "I'll take one shift," Carmen said.

"I'll take the other one," Denise replied.

"Thanks, ladies— when you get a chance, come to my office to sign the overtime book."

"Carmen, did you forget that you want to sleep in tomorrow?"

"I know, but I can't pass up overtime money. You know, some may say all money isn't good money, but I say overtime money is great money!" "I agree," Denise laughs.

"Denise, please remind me to call Latoya to let her know that I'm not dropping by tonight."

"Sure, I got you covered. Anyway, Latoya might be asleep, exhausted from traveling; you may want to call her now.

"Okay, cover for me."

Where did I put my phone? It's not in my locker; don't tell me I've lost my phone? There it is. I hope Latoya answers. No answer: she must be asleep, thought Carmen.

"Hey, Latoya, I accepted overtime for tomorrow morning, so I'll take a ring check on dropping by — Call me tomorrow—have a blessed night. Denise, I am back; thanks for covering for me."

"Did you talk to her?"

"No, but I left a message."

"I was just thinking she may still be driving home.

"You might be right. Anyway, it's almost quitting time. Do you need a break before I check out?"

"I do, thanks, Carmen; I haven't been feeling well all day."

"Neither have I."

"Do you have any snacks?"

"Are you still hungry? Look in my locker; I might have some potato chips. Whatever is in there is yours.

"Are you sure you're okay.

"Yes, just a little tired."

* * *

The night was surprisingly calm as Latoya pulled into her driveway, but her heart skipped a beat when she spotted a stunning surprise— thirty-six long-stemmed lavender and white roses waiting at her front door.

A mix of confusion and delight washed over her as she bent down to grab them.

"Mamma Mia, what beautiful roses!" she said aloud, her voice a mix of excitement and disbelief. Inside, she wasted no time and pulled out her phone, eager to share the news with Carmen.

"Hello?"

"Carmen, you're not going to believe this! I just came home to see thirty-six purple and white long-stem roses!" Latoya's words tumbled out, overflowing with enthusiasm. "And there's a card that says, 'secret admirer!' I can't even process this!"

"Whoa! Do you think it's your 'pink bicycle date' from Atlanta?" Carmen jokes, her voice layered with a hint of skepticism mixed with intrigue.

"Right? It has to be him! Who else would send thirty-six roses to my door?" Latoya could hardly contain her excitement. Carmen's tone shifted slightly.

"Are you sure? I thought you didn't share your address with guys you meet online." Latoya paused, the realization hitting her.

"You're totally right! I didn't! So, if it's not him, then who on earth could it be?" She laughed, trying to lighten the moment.

"I have no idea, but please just lock your doors tonight. Let's chat more about it tomorrow," Carmen urged, a protective edge to her voice.

"Alright, I'll do that. Goodnight!" her mind buzzing with possibilities as she hung up.

The mystery of the roses danced through her thoughts as she made her way to her bedroom, a peaceful oasis with crisp, white Egyptian cotton sheets and a cozy knit throw draped over the bed.

"So, is this how it feels to receive flowers from a secret admirer? I can get used to this. I need to lie down and go to sleep, and in the morning, when Carmen and I talk again, she will tell me what to do," Latoya said to herself.

Carefully, she set the roses on her nightstand, flopped onto her bed, fluffed her pillows to raise her head high enough to keep her eyes on the roses, and pulled up her dating app, ready to see who else might be out there waiting for her next adventure.

The next morning, the airport teemed with life; rows of standard airport chairs lined the waiting area. Travelers filled the seats, some animatedly chatting while others stared blankly at their phones. A child lay sprawled asleep, his backpack serving as a pillow. Latoya handed her boarding pass to the gate agent, ready to board the plane to Atlanta.

At the ticket counter, Denise and Carmen are working briskly to check in passengers. At that moment, Carmen's phone rang, and she stepped away from the counter to answer.

"Hello."

"Hey, it's me, Latoya," came the voice on the other end. "I'm on my way to Atlanta, and before you say anything, no, it's not the same guy." Carmen frowned as she held the phone to her ear, her mind still racing with questions.

"That's not what I want to know," she muttered, glancing around the busy ticket counter. She had just learned that Latoya was off for the day, and it threw her off-kilter. "I didn't know you were off today."

"I cleared it with the supervisor last night. Anyway, not to cut you off, the doors to the plane are closing. I will call you when I land. Luv ya." With a sigh, Carmen rushed back to the ticket counter, where the atmosphere was thick with the energy of customers waiting impatiently in line.

"Where is Latoya? Shouldn't she be at work? She still works here, right?" Denise inquired.

Carmen replied with a hint of annoyance.

"Latoya is off today; in fact, she's on her way to Atlanta. And can you tell me why you are in such a bad mood? Do you need a break?"

Denise, undeterred, replied, "No, I don't need a break, but if you insist."

"I insist."

Without hesitation, Denise rushed over and wrapped Carmen in a tight hug.

"Fine, I'll go. I'm ordering Chinese food — care for anything?"

"Yes, order me whatever you're having," resigning to her friend's whims.

"Okay. The house fried rice, baby back ribs, and a side of steamed broccoli make it large," Denise declared with determination.

"Never mine! That is too much food for one person. Are you seriously going to eat all of that? Carmen shot incredulously.

"Absolutely. You know I love Chinese food," Denise said, pulling out her phone to place the order.

"Speaking of help, here come the two new hires," Carmen noted as the new employees approached the counter, flanked by the supervisor. "Good, I'll go pick up the order," Denise said before quickly walking towards the exit.

"Denise, wait for me!" Carmen called, rushing after her friend.

In the food court, Denise and Carmen settled at a table, the menu clutched in Denise's hands. A young waiter approached them with a friendly smile.

"What can I get for you ladies?"

"I called in my order, but for my friend here, she will have a cheeseburger with everything... and fries, a Coke, extra-large. And don't forget the apple pie," Denise instructed, glancing at Carmen with a mischievous smile.

Carmen raised an eyebrow in mock disbelief.

"Did you just order for me?"

"Yes, I did. I'm just making sure you don't starve," Denise replied cheekily.

The waiter took the menu from Carmen and disappeared back into the bustling food court.

Denise leaned in conspiratorially, her grin widening.

"So, what did you and Latoya talk about last night?" "Oh, I almost forgot!" Carmen responded, her eyes sparkling with intrigue. "Latoya has a secret admirer. He sent thirty-six long-stem purple and white roses to her house."

"Thirty-six roses? Wow," Denise exclaimed, leaning back in her chair as if the impact were tangible. The waiter returned with their food and placed the platters in the center of the table. Denise, not one to wait, reached for Carmen's cheeseburger, took a large bite, and grabbed two fries to nibble on.

"You wouldn't have any idea who sent the roses, right?"

Denise shrugged, her mouth full of fries,

"Roses! How did Latoya respond?"

Carmen gave Denise a pointed look as she chewed with her mouth open.

"Well—she was excited, and she thinks they're from her online date."

"Who? Pink two-seater bicycle—Nope, I don't think they were from him," Denise argued, shaking her head.

"Neither do I. Give me some of your Chinese rice since you ate my burger and fries," Carmen retorted, rolling her eyes but unable to hide her amusement.

* * *

As the hours passed, the arrival at Gate 4 buzzed with anticipation as the flight from Atlanta landed. A crowd eagerly awaited the passengers, and soon Latoya emerged, her head lowered, and her eyes fixed ahead. She walked briskly, hurrying to the parking lot, where her car awaited. Latoya unlocked the door, tossed her luggage into the backseat, and turned on the music, filling the car with her favorite tunes as she drove home.

Pulling into her driveway, she spotted another package on her doorstep.

"What now?" she muttered to herself, curiously approaching the package. With a glance around, she reached down and picked it up. Inside her cozy olive-green kitchen, she dropped her keys on the table and shook the box.

"Okay, whoever this is... You really got my attention, "she said to herself. Unpacking the box, Latoya's heart raced as she pulled out front-row concert tickets and a

dinner reservation at Maggiano's Little Italy. Excitement coursed through her veins. Dropping the tickets, she

fished her iPhone out of her purse and hastily dialed Carmen.

"Hello?"

"Hey! Carmen, you are not going to believe this.

I have another package at my front door." "Another package? What's in it?" Carmen asked eagerly. Latoya's words tumbled out.

"Front-row concert tickets and dinner reservation at my favorite restaurant, Maggiano's

Little Italy!"

"Say no more, I'm coming over as soon as my shift ends," her enthusiasm matching Latoya's.

"Hurry!" Latoya urged, a grin stretching across her face as she anticipated Carmen's arrival.

Carmen fastened her seatbelt and drove off into the night, her destination the Italian Pizza House. After a quick stop, she emerged with a large pepperoni pizza in hand.

Once back in her car, she continued her journey to Latoya's house, anticipation simmering inside her.

Meanwhile, inside Denise's home, the atmosphere was heavy with sorrow. Denise sat on her bed, tears streaming down her cheeks, her gaze fixed on an old wedding photo of her parents. She reminisced about her childhood, a time before the foster homes changed everything.

Denise picked up her iPhone, her fingers trembling slightly as she dialed Carmen's number. She placed the phone against her ear, the sound of it ringing filling the silence around her.

"Hello?" came Carmen's voice, muffled slightly as she turned the car radio down. "Carmen—where are you?" Denise's voice was urgent, laced with a hint of curiosity.

"I'm driving to Latoya's house," Carmen replied, a hint of excitement creeping into her tone. "She got another package from her secret admirer."

"Really. Good for her," Denise said, her voice flat, almost detached.

"Uhm. Are you okay?" Carmen sensed something was off. Denise rubbed her eyes with the back of her hand, trying to blink away the remnants of her earlier thoughts.

"I've been better," she admitted, her gaze shifting to the photo once more before she flipped it over and tucked it into a drawer. "When you get to Latoya's, FaceTime me so I can hear all about the new package she received," Denise requested, her tone shifting as she embraced the distraction.

"Okay! Will do. And you sure you're okay?"

"Yes, I'm okay," Denise lied, her heart heavy with unspoken feelings as the call ended.

Carmen turned up the radio once more, losing herself in the music as she drove toward Latoya's house. Denise lay back on her bed, waiting for the FaceTime call, her mind swirling with thoughts.

Arriving at Latoya's house, Carmen pulled into the driveway and exited her car, carefully balancing the pizza in her arms. Latoya rushed to greet her, flinging open the front door.

"Hurry…get in here!" Latoya's excitement was evident.

"Careful! Don't make me drop the pizza!" Carmen teased, holding it high.

Inside, the living room radiated warmth and style, with a deep blue plush sofa and a matching armchair, a round wooden center table, and a stucco accent wall that added a touch of sophistication to the hardwood floors.

Latoya jumped with excitement, snatching the pizza from Carmen's hands. She plopped down on the sofa, throwing the box open and immediately grabbing a slice.

"The excitement is killing me! Have a seat next to me," she laughed, her eyes sparkling with delight. "Wait, I almost

forgot! Denise wants me to FaceTime her so she can be a part of this," Carmen remembered, reaching for her phone again, then dials Denise's number. She connected to FaceTime. Holding her phone so that Latoya could see Denise.

"Are you there?" Carmen asked as Denise's FaceTime beeped, the screen flashing with Denise's image.

"Hey…I can see you both," sitting up in her bed, okay, please help me out here: roses, concert tickets, and dinner reservations. Who is this person?"

"Someone who really wants to get to know you better," Carmen offered, a teasing tone in her voice.

"Come on, Latoya, no man is sending all that unless he has strong feelings for you. Think about it," Denise added, her own feelings tangled in the words.

Carmen raised eyebrows, "Yes, we know that much, but the question is—who?"

Latoya took a hearty bite of her pizza, wiping her mouth with a napkin.

"I'm curious about all of this. What is it that he really wants?"

"Not to sound pessimistic," Carmen said, glancing at Latoya, "but this person must know you or know someone who knows you." Denise shook her head slightly, "Not really." "Well, I think so," Carmen replied.

"Latoya, just be careful." The night wore on, and Denise felt a wave of fatigue washing over her.

"Ladies, it's late. I say we sleep on it and talk more tomorrow." Carmen disconnected the FaceTime call, leaving the screen's glow behind. She gathered her things, said her goodbyes, and stepped back into the cool night air, the weight of the evening lingering in her thoughts as she drove home.

# Chapter 3

It was just another busy Monday morning at the Herself Airline ticket counter, but for Denise and Carmen, it felt like the start of something fun. The smell of coffee and fresh bread wafted through the air, mixing with the sounds of crying babies and hurried porters. Long lines were wrapping around the counters, but amidst the chaos, they were in their own little bubble.

"Good morning, Carmen!" Denise called out, grinning from ear to ear.

"Morning, Denise! Ready to dive into this crazy day?" Carmen shot back, her energy brightening the space around them.

Denise laughed, "Not until I've had my first cup of go-getter!" They both knew how vital that morning coffee was for Denise's vibe.

"I'm telling you, today's going to be a blast!" Carmen said, her excitement bubbling over. "What's the flight load look like? Are we all booked up?"  "Yep! Full house today, just the way we like it," Denise replied, her enthusiasm matching Carmen's.

After hours of checking in passengers, a voice comes over the announcement system, echoing through the terminal, "May I have your attention, please? Denise Morgan, you are needed at the main entrance of the airport terminal for an important message."

Denise paused, uncertain whether the announcement referred to her or another Denise Morgan. Curiosity nudged her to find out. She slowly walked over to the front entrance of the airport. As she approached the door, Carmen reached out and pulled her through the door.

"Get over here, Denise," Carmen whispered.

"What is going on? I was afraid to come over here."

"I want you to see this with your own eyes."

"See what?" Denise asked. "What is it?"

"Look— in that blue car," Carmen pointed.

"Luscious Lyon!" Denise screamed. "Luscious, where is Cookie?"

"Control yourself, Denise—remember you're in uniform," Carmen chastised softly. "I should have known better; the lust she has for that man."

"Marry me, Luscious!" Denise shouted, her excitement taking over.

"That's it, you have lost your mind. It is time to go back to work." Carmen took Denise by the hand and yanked her back inside the airport. "It's my fault; I should have known better."

"I am in heaven—thank you, Carmen, it was a wonderful surprise. I won't forget this day," Denise smiled as they returned to the ticket counter.

"Hey, Denise and Carmen, the boss is looking for you two," a co-worker said.

"Why? Do you know why?" Carmen asked softly.

"You didn't hear this from me, but something about misuse of the airport paging system."

"Snap!" Carmen exclaimed. "Let me talk to her; you don't need to come, Denise."

"Yes—I do. She asked for me too—I'm coming with you."

"But you didn't do anything wrong. If anyone is going to get into trouble, let it be me."

"I insist; no more negotiation. Besides, we are unsure why she wants to see us. It could be anything."

"You're right," Carmen conceded. "Let's go to her office and get it over with."

"Boss, you need to see us?" Carmen asked as they entered.

"Get in here and close the door!" the Supervisor ordered.

"Yes, ma'am," Carmen replied.

"Do you need me?" Denise asked softly.

"No, I need Carmen."

"Okay, I'll be at the ticket counter."

"Close the door, please. Carmen, do you know why you are in my office?"

"No, ma'am, I don't."

"Would you like to guess why you are here?"

"No ma'am."

"I will tell you anyway; did you make an airport page for Denise?"

"Yes—I did," Carmen sighed. "I want to apologize for doing that. I should not have done that, and I am sorry I did."

"You better not do it again. Go on, get out of here."

"Thank you." Carmen felt relief wash over her. "Thank you, Lord Jesus, for allowing me to keep my job," she thought. "Carmen, what happened?"

"I will tell you later; I need to work right now. Next passenger in line, please. Where are you traveling to today?" Carmen said.

"Here is my itinerary; I'm checking two bags."

"Yes, sir, here is your boarding pass and bag claims. Thank you. Next in line, please—hello, how may I help you?"

"So, you're not going to tell me what happened?"

"Denise, can you not see me with a passenger?"

"Excuse me for wanting to know what happened."

"I need to check in, please," a passenger requested.

"Yes, sir, here is your boarding pass. Are you checking bags this evening?" "One," he replied.

"Okay, you're all checked in; however, your flight is a little delayed, about fifteen minutes.
Anything else?
"No, that will be all."

Denise turns to Carmen, "Now, can you tell me what was said and what happened in there?

"Nothing went on—nobody said anything, are you satisfied?
"No."

"I said that I was sorry for misusing the paging system. Then, I got instructions not to do it again." "Okay, so you good?" Denise asked, concerned.
"Yes."
"I was thinking you were in trouble, and I knew I was the cause of your actions."

"No, I am responsible for my own actions— not you. The good news is, it's all over, and I still have a job. Thank you, God!"

"Amen!" Denise replied.

"I need a break; can you cover the ticket counter while I take a minute?"
"Yes—go take all the time you need."
"Thanks."

"But, when you get back from break, I want to tell you about Max Jones.

"Where is Carmen?" the supervisor asked.

"She stepped away for a moment, but should be back soon.

"Okay, let her know I need to see her again," and no, she's not in any trouble.

Only moments had passed, and Carmen walked by.

"Go see the supervisor. Don't worry; you're not in any trouble."

"Don't scare me like that. I wonder what it is now?"

"I can go in with you if you like."

"Sure, why not?"

"No. I was kidding," Denise laughed.

"What a friend," Carmen said with a smile as she entered the supervisor's office.

"I have an overtime shift for tomorrow, four hours from 9 a.m. to 1 p.m., would you like it?

"Yes, I'll take it."

"Okay, you're free to go.

"Thanks," she smiled as she left the office.

"What was it?" Denise asked.

"Over time tomorrow from 9 a.m. until 12 noon, and I could use the money. And what's the news about Max moving back to Florida, and why should I care?"

"I'm not sure if you should care, but yes, he is moving back. I heard he is single, so he's coming back alone."

"Okay, and?" Carmen pressed.

"Nothing, I just wanted to tell you that."

"Please tell me if there is more. I know there must be more because you're too excited to share just that. What else?"

"Here's my thought: if we get Latoya and Max back together, she might rethink having a baby with a stranger."

Carmen objected, "Oh no, I do not play matchmaker. I have no interest in this. Anyway, I thought you liked Max."

"No! He's one of the most charming and stylish men I've seen lately, but he's not my type. I want you to consider this: we can help our friend."

"I want to go on record that I do not think this is a good idea. It's interesting, but not good. Latoya has made it clear that she isn't looking for a relationship or marriage; she wants a child," Carmen stated firmly.

"I know, and that sounds crazier every time I hear it. Just let me work my magic; all I need from you is not to say anything to Latoya."

"Don't worry, I won't. And, again, is Max not Latoya's ex-husband? And why is he so important to you?"

"He's not—I didn't say he was important to me."

"Well, it surely sounds that way. Anyway, I'm taking my break

*Is it that obvious? Our only real interaction happened six months ago. He's probably forgotten all about it. But I haven't, and I know I never will. To this day, I can never.*

*Shake the connection I felt between Max and the magic of that night,* Denise remembers.

# Chapter 4

Latoya, Denise, and Carmen busied themselves at the airline ticket counter, the morning bustle of travelers creating a steady rhythm around them. The air was filled with announcements and the sound of rolling luggage, blending into a familiar symphony of airport life.

"Next in line, please!" Denise's voice rang out, precise and unwavering. Just as Latoya stepped away from the counter, a figure entered the scene, drawing her attention. It was Timothy James, a pilot for Aruba Airlines in his thirties and an old friend of Denise's. He removed his hat and approached with a warm smile.

"Hello, Denise," he greeted.

But she didn't acknowledge him. Her focus remained on checking in the passengers, her movements as sharp as her demeanor.

"Good morning, Denise Timothy tried again, a hint of disappointment creeping into his voice. She glanced briefly

in his direction, then returned to the queue of travelers. Carmen, who had noticed Timothy's struggle for attention, stepped in.

"Sir, I can help you over here," she offered

"Oh no," Timothy replied, shaking his head.

"I'm not checking in, just hoping to speak with Denise."

Max, another Aruba Airlines pilot and a familiar face for both Denise and Latoya, approached Timothy. He extended a hand to Timothy.

"You're Timothy James? How long has it been?" Max exclaimed, genuinely pleased to see his old friend.

"Max? Man, good to see you... It's been ages.

Last time I remember, it was at our Pilot Annual

Holiday party at the Ritz Carlton Resort."

"That's right! What brings you here?" Max inquired, curiosity sparking in his eyes just as Denise walked over, prompted by the familiar voices.

"Hello, Max. Thank you for this." He handed her an envelope, and she accepted it with a steady voice.

"I will be sure she gets it."

"Thanks, Denise." Max smiled before turning back to Timothy. Just as quickly, Denise returned to the ticket counter, a sense of finality in her motions. "What's going on with you two?" Max asked Timothy, intrigued by the tension he had just witnessed.

"How do you know Denise?

"She's a friend of my ex-wife, Latoya. And I'll let you in on a secret: Denise is helping me out— I'm trying to win Latoya back."

"No kidding. I'm trying to do something similar with Denise," Timothy confessed, hope flickering in his eyes.

"Really? You and Denise? Let me know if I can help in any way."

They exchanged numbers, parting ways with an unspoken understanding before returning to their respective tasks.

Back at the ticket counter, the atmosphere remained relaxed. Passengers moved through at a comfortable pace while the airline staff, clad in crisp uniforms, maintained their cheerful composure.

Latoya returned just as Denise handed her an envelope.

"Here, open this. It has your name on it," her tone mixing mystery with enthusiasm.

"For me?" Latoya exclaimed, surprise dancing in her eyes as she tore open the envelope.

"It's an RSVP for dinner Saturday night!" she read aloud, her curiosity piqued. Carmen, who had been eavesdropping, walked over, intrigued. "Let me see this. Dinner reservation at 6 p.m. Saturday."

Inquisitively, Denise asked, "Are you going?"

"I'm not sure," Latoya admitted, clutching the envelope as she moved to the far end of the counter, her mind racing with possibilities.

Outside the terminal, a young UPS courier, dressed in a standard uniform, approached the ticket counter, clutching roses in his hands.

"I'm looking for a Latoya Marino," he announced, scanning the counter.

"I'm Latoya Marino," she said, confusion knitting her brows as he presented three dozen lavender and white roses, accompanied by a box of Godiva chocolates.

"Great! Sign here," he insisted, his delivery professional yet hurried. Latoya, flustered, instantly signed out and departed the counter, the flowers cradled in her arms. Carmen sat opposite Denise at a small table. Latoya burst in, bouquet in hand, clearly agitated.

"Okay, this is over the top—more roses and more candy. Who is this guy?" she exclaimed breathlessly.

"Well, if you go to dinner, you might just find out," Denise suggested playfully, a hint of mischief in her voice.

Carmen shook her head slowly, eyes wide in disbelief.

"I can't believe I'm agreeing with Denise, but she's right."

As they walked back to the ticket counter, Timothy reentered the scene, and Denise, taken aback, approached him.

"Timothy, what do you want?" she demanded, her hands flailing as she tried to maintain her composure amid the chaos. "I promise, if you don't leave and never come back..." she started, her frustration discernible.

Timothy's expression shifted to a serious one.

"What? What are you going to do? Denise— we need to talk."

Denise turned away, determined, "I have nothing to say to you."

Carmen drifted closer, sensing the tension that hung in the air.

"Denise, are you okay?" she asked, her protective instincts kicking in.

"I'm okay," Denise replied curtly, but Carmen eyed her knowingly, sensing something was amiss. With firm resolve, Denise pushed past Carmen and walked outside to confront Timothy.

"Okay, Timothy, what do you have to say?" she demanded, stepping up to him with fiery determination. The tension thickened the air as two pasts collided, leaving the future uncertain and tangled in desires yet to be revealed.

Timothy's heart raced as his eyes locked onto Denise.

"When were you going to tell me about the baby?" he asked, his voice barely concealing the whirlwind of emotions inside him.

"Baby? What baby?"

"I'm not playing games here," Timothy insisted, desperation creeping into his tone. "I just want to be a part of my child's life." Denise stepped closer, her gaze unwavering, the bravado hiding her vulnerability.

"Timothy, you are not the father of my baby."

"I don't believe you," he shot back, frustration evident as his thoughts raced. "You can't just drop a bomb like this and expect me to walk away."

"For the last time, you are not the father!" Denise asserted, her voice firm, yet a hint of uncertainty flared within her. She turned on her heel, leaving Timothy standing alone in disbelief.

As the night wore on, the airport buzzed with passengers checking in. Denise returned to her duties, her earlier encounter with Timothy still weighing heavily on her heart.

Under the warm lights of the food court and the alluring scent of fries, Latoya and Carmen discussed their lives.

"What are you thinking?" Carmen asked, aware of Latoya's inner turmoil.

"I'm not sure if I should go to dinner," her heart heavy with uncertainty about the choices ahead.

"Yes, I think you should go," she said, her encouraging smile lighting up her face.

After placing her order, Latoya sat down at a small table with Carmen. As they ate, Latoya's smile caught Carmen off guard.

"What's the grin for?"

"Okay, I confess… it feels good to be noticed," Latoya said playfully, making Carmen laugh. As night fell, Denise continued checking in passengers, trying to focus on her

work. Latoya and Carmen approached her; their energy was infectious.

"How was lunch?" Denise asked, trying to maintain her composure.

"Delicious! A much-needed break," Latoya cheerfully declared.

Denise glanced at the clock, "It's time for me to go. Remember, it's Saturday; the counter closes early," she said, attempting to shake the weight of her earlier conversation from her mind.

Later that night, Denise drove her dark grey Nissan Maximus into Carmen's driveway, the quiet night amplifying the chaos in her heart. She knocked urgently on the front door. Carmen opened it, surprised.

"Denise? What's going on?" Inside, the atmosphere shifted.

"I need to talk!" Denise exclaimed, urgency slipping through her voice. Carmen hurried to grab two glasses and a bottle of wine, sensing the gravity behind Denise's anxious demeanor. As the glasses filled, Denise took a deep breath, struggling with the weight of her confession.

"I'm *pregnant!*" she finally blurted out, her voice trembling. Carmen's eyes widened in shock.

"*Pregnant!*" she echoed, the tension thick in the air. "Do you know who the father is?"

Denise hesitated, "I'm not sure," the words left her lips heavy with uncertainty.

"Is it Timothy?" Carmen's concern was evident, and Denise felt the tears starting to slip.

"I... I don't know. He thinks he is," Denise finally admitted, her dread etched in her features. "And I'm not sure if I'm going to keep the baby." Carmen stepped closer, her heart aching for her friend.

"What do you mean by 'if you're keeping the baby?' You have to think this through."

"Please, Carmen, don't judge me!" Denise turned away, her back facing Carmen in a moment of vulnerability.

"Stop! Don't leave. I'm not judging you. I want to help," Carmen pleaded.

Denise shook her head, feeling the load of her choices crashing down on her.

"I can't have this baby," she whispered, her voice breaking under the weight of desperation.

Carmen's heart ached as she wrapped her arms around Denise and pulled her close.

"You're not alone in this. I promise you, whatever you decide, I'll be by your side."

Denise sobbed quietly; a flicker of resolve ignited within her. In the dim light of Carmen's kitchen, surrounded by the warmth of friendship, she felt a strength she didn't know she possessed. Perhaps the unexpected path ahead holds more than fear and uncertainty—maybe it leads to love, connection, and even healing.

Outside, the world continued to turn, but in that moment, Denise understood that choices might not just shape her future; they might also lead to deeper bonds and unforeseen connections. The journey was only beginning. Denise wiped her eyes, still feeling the sting of tears as she faced the looming uncertainty of her next steps. With a heavy heart, she turned the knob on the front door, hesitating a moment before glancing back at Carmen.

"I don't know about all that, but please don't tell anyone about this—especially Latoya," Denise urged, the urgency in her voice betraying her fear.

Carmen rushed forward and enveloped her in another warm embrace, trying to convey all the support she felt.

"Okay, but you don't have to decide anything right now. Just stay the night," she offered, concern etched on her face. Denise shook her head vigorously.

"No. I'll be okay. Plus, I have a doctor's appointment in the morning. Can we see each other tomorrow?" The worry in Carmen's eyes deepened as she replied,

"Yes. I love you, Denise. Please drive safely."

Denise stepped out; the weight pressing down on her intensified with every step. After the door clicked shut,

Latoya settled onto the sofa, her mind racing with the evening's events.

The next day, at the ticket counter, the airport buzzed with the chatter of travelers, but all Latoya could think of was Denise.

Carmen and Latoya worked diligently, yet Carmen kept glancing at the entrance, her heart pounding with impatience. When Denise finally came into work, she was accompanied by a sense of dread.

"Hey, everyone, I'm here," Denise's voice rang out, but it carried a hint of frustration that set off alarm bells in Carmen's mind.

"Sorry, I'm late. I was stuck in traffic, a three-car pileup on I-95." Denise's irritation was visible, and Carmen felt her own worry mount.

"Denise, I need to see you in my office," the supervisor called out, and Denise's heart sank.

"Yes, boss. On my way," she managed to reply, bracing for the worst. When the supervisor delivered the news, the cold reality hit Denise hard.

"This is your third time being late this month. Please sign this attendance letter; it's your final warning." Denise sighed, the weight of the world pressing down on her chest.

"I know, I should've planned better. I'm really sorry, but the accident was completely unexpected," she pleaded, hoping for a flicker of understanding. "It's unfortunate for you," the supervisor replied curtly.

With a heavy heart, Denise signed the letter, knowing the stakes had just risen. As she stepped back into the bustling airport, she felt like the walls were closing in around her.

# Chapter 5

In the busy airline ticket counter, Carmen and Latoya were working hard, checking in passengers like pros. Their day was rolling along as usual when Denise walked up, looking determined.

"Carmen, go take a break," Denise said, her tone making it clear it wasn't up for debate. Carmen nodded gratefully and stepped away, feeling like she needed a little breather after a long morning. Latoya approached Denise, practically bouncing with excitement.

"Ciao, today is my big day!" Latoya exclaimed, her voice full of energy. "Can you come help me get dressed?"

"Of course! I'd love to," Denise replied, smiling brightly.

"Thanks, Denise, you're the best!" Latoya said, her eyes sparkling with enthusiasm.

"No problem—let's aim for around four this afternoon," Denise suggested, happy to help her out. Latoya skipped away, leaving a trail of excitement behind her.

Carmen returned from her quick lunch, her hands full as she made her way back to Denise.

"Thanks, Carmen!" Denise said as she took the lunch bag, feeling revitalized.

"It all makes sense now that I know. Where is Latoya?"

"She left. Remember, it's her date night," Denise reminded her.

"Right," Carmen sighed, then turned to Denise.

"So, how are you doing?"

"Health-wise, I'm okay," Denise admitted, her smile fading a bit. "But emotionally? Not great. Plus, I just got a final warning for attendance."

The heaviness of her struggles lingered between them. Carmen reached out, taking Denise's hands in hers. She squeezed them gently and closed her eyes, getting ready for a quiet prayer.

"Dear Lord, help Denise trust Your plan. Give her strength and peace during this tough time.

Amen."

"Amen," Denise echoed softly, feeling the warmth of Carmen's support.

"You know, Denise, my shift is wrapping up now," Carmen said after a moment. "I could really use some extra

hours, so let me cover your last four hours, and you can go help Latoya."

"Really? Thank you so much, Carmen! I owe you!"

****

In Max's cluttered bedroom, he felt that his life was chaotic. Clothes were strewn across his unmade bed, jazz posters covered the gray walls, and a grandfather clock ticked softly in the corner. Just as he started to get lost in his thoughts, his iPhone rang, pulling him back to reality.
"Hello?"

"Max, I need to talk," Timothy said, sounding urgent and upset.

Max stopped dancing around and turned the music down, "I'm all ears."

"Have you ever gotten your heart ripped out with just four words?" Timothy asked, his voice heavy with emotion.

Max frowned, thinking it over, "I don't know about just four words. I've been divorced and know what it's like to have your heart broken."
"Four words, Max. Four words ruined me."
"What four words?"

"It's not your baby," Timothy said, the pain clear even through the phone. Max shifted the phone to the other ear and sat on the edge of his bed, feeling for his friend.

"Listen, man, I don't want to sound insensitive, but, hey, at least you found out before getting too invested in something that's not yours."

"If you can call that a bright side…" Timothy shot back, his sarcasm barely hiding the hurt. "Well, thanks for listening."

"Seriously, man, if you need to talk, I'm always here," Max reassured him, hoping to be a solid friend. Timothy hung up. Max took a deep breath, feeling the weight of their conversation hanging in the air around him.

* * *

In a trendy nail and hair salon filled with soft music and modern decor, Latoya lounged in a brown high-back chair, surrounded by the smell of nail polish. A nail tech applied a fresh coat to her fingers while Latoya excitedly shared all about the romantic surprises she had received.

"He sent thirty-six purple and white roses and chocolate to my job!" she gushed.

"Purple and white roses?" the nail tech asked, intrigued. "Did you know purple roses symbolize enchantment and love, while white roses stand for innocence and new beginnings?"

"No way, I didn't know that!" Latoya replied, her smile was growing wider. The thought made her heart race. "Plus, he got us front-row seats to a jazz concert!"

"Wow, you're in for a treat! What do you think of your nails? They're purple and white, just like your roses," the nail tech added, admiring her work.

Latoya held up her hands, checking out the color.

"They look amazing. Thanks so much!"

After paying the nail tech, she wrapped her arms around her for a warm hug before leaving the salon, excitement bubbling up inside her.

Latoya is now in her bedroom, the atmosphere radiated romance, softened by warm lighting and pastel walls. The elegant bed, adorned with plush pillows, contrasted with the stylish closet that revealed her passion for fashion.

Yet, a weight hung in the air. Latoya and Denise rummaged through the closet, the undercurrent of tension visible. Denise's fingers trembled slightly as she glanced at her watch, anxiety flickering in her eyes.

"Wear this one!" Denise exclaimed, holding up a sleek black midriff dress that shimmered softly under the lighting.

"Do you really think so?" Latoya asked, doubt lacing her voice. Stepping closer, Denise offered heartfelt encouragement.

"You're beautiful, Latoya. You have to believe it."

Gratitude shone in Latoya's eyes, but a deeper layer of vulnerability lay hidden beneath the surface. She embraced Denise tightly, attempting to absorb her strength.

"Thanks, Denise. I don't know what I'd do without you," Latoya admitted, her voice thick with emotion.

Denise held her tight in response, their shared warmth offering comfort against the backdrop of their struggles.

"You're not alone. I promise," Denise assured her.

They finally pulled apart, tears glistened in Latoya's eyes, overwhelmed by the moment. She smiled at Denise, but her voice trembled, signaling the weight of her fear and uncertainty.

"I'll call you later," she managed to say, the ties of friendship fortifying her spirit as the evening's promise unfolded. Taking a moment to absorb Denise's comforting presence, Latoya watched her friend linger in the hallway.

As Denise's footsteps faded, a sense of solitude washed over Latoya, piercing her heart with a blend of hope and fear. Once the door clicked shut behind Denise, she hurried to get dressed for her date.

Inside Maggiano's that night, soft, ambient lighting created an inviting atmosphere. Candlelit tables shone softly, twinkling string lights hung overhead, and plush seating surrounded fresh floral arrangements.

The gentle notes of music floated through the air as Latoya sat at her reserved table, fidgeting with her napkin while glancing at her watch too often.

She tapped her fingers rhythmically on the table, took a deep breath, and scanned the room, her gaze anxiously darting toward the entrance. Moments later, a waiter in his thirties approached her table, balancing a glass of water with lemon.

"Water with lemon for the beautiful lady," he said, a warm smile gracing his face.

Latoya looked up from her menu, surprise flickering across her features as her cheeks colored slightly upon meeting the waiter's gaze. "Max!" she shouts, recognizing him.

"I am your waiter, so will you be dining alone?" he replied, leaning in slightly, curiosity alight in his eyes. "No, I'm on a blind date. Well, not exactly blind—

I know him, thanks to the gifts he's given me." Max, intrigued, took a seat across from her.

"So, a blind date. Tell me, what are you most looking forward to?"

Latoya found herself momentarily speechless, folding her napkin into the shape of an airplane as her heart raced.

"Forgive me if I'm making you nervous."

She pulled out a small mirror and a tube of lipstick, freshening her lips as she struggled to steady her breath.

"Max, stop with the questions, please; you are making me nervous."

"Again, I apologize. I wish you good luck on your date," he said, standing and leaving her with her thoughts.

Alone at the table, Latoya's nerves vibrated through her as she glanced around. The familiar scent of Blue Jean cologne wafted through the air, evoking distant memories.

Her attention snapped to a figure entering the restaurant: a man in a sleek black tuxedo walked toward her, his gait

oddly familiar, holding a single long-stem rose in his right hand.

"Good evening, Latoya," he greeted, his voice smooth.

Latoya froze, her breath hitching.

"Max, are you...?"

"Yes, I am your date," he confirmed, a playful smirk forming on his lips.

Motionless, Latoya took a sip of her water as Max pulled out the chair opposite her. He signaled to the waiter, who arrived promptly.

"Yes, what can I get for you?" the waiter inquired.

"Bring over a bottle of champagne," Max ordered confidently.

"Certainly, right away, sir."

Latoya leaned back in her chair, her heart racing. Words failed her, leaving her in a sea of confusion as Max studied her intently.

"It's okay. I know it's a lot to take in," he reassured her, his gaze steady.

"You think?" Latoya managed, her voice tinged with disbelief.

The waiter returned, placing a bottle of Dom Perignon and two glasses on the table before pouring the champagne.

"Will there be anything else?" he asked after setting the bottle down.

Without waiting for Max, Latoya downed a big gulp from her glass.

"I'm going to need something a little stronger than this." Max turned to the waiter.

"Bring the lady a shot of Patron tequila."

"A double shot, please."

The evening was filled with surprises, and Latoya felt the thrill of possibilities dancing in the air around them. Latoya leaned back in her chair, a soft chuckle escaping her lips as she pieced together the surprises.

"I should have known—the roses! The Kenny

G concert tickets! And my favorite restaurant,

Maggiano's! No one else could have known."

The waiter arrived swiftly, placing a double shot of Patron on the table before asking, "Are you ready to order?"

With confidence, Latoya replied, "Shrimp scaloppine, with all the fixings." She glanced at Max, who, after a brief moment, mirrored her choice.

"I will have the same," he said, with a playful smile creeping onto his face. The waiter nodded and left them alone, the quiet around them thick with anticipation. Max leaned forward, his expression shifting to one of earnestness.

"Tell me, Latoya, how do you feel?"

"Honestly, Max... I don't know what I feel," she admitted, her heart a swirl of confusion and excitement.

"Okay. Come—go with me. I want to show you something." He stood and extended his hand out. Latoya

hesitated for a moment, her arms crossed, but curiosity edged out her doubts. Taking his hand, she felt a spark of connection that sent warmth through her.

Together, they climbed a small flight of stairs. When they reached the rooftop of Maggiano's, the scene transformed into a magical haven—soft lights shimmered around them, and flickering candles created a cozy ambiance. The plush seating and fresh flowers added to the enchantment, while a chilled bottle of champagne awaited them. "Now that you know it's me, do you want to continue the date and go to the concert?" Max asked, anticipation shining in his eyes.

Latoya's face lit up, her gaze sparkling like stars in the twilight sky.

"Since you already have the tickets, and Kenny G is still my all-time favorite jazz artist, I guess we can," she replied, feeling her heart settle into a rhythm of excitement. The waiter served their food, and Max took Latoya's hand, offering a prayer over their meal.

"Thank you, God, for this good food and for better company. In Jesus' name, Amen!"

"Amen," Latoya echoed, her heart swelling with the warmth of connection. Laughter and chatter flowed. They enjoyed their meal; the thrill of the evening's events hung in the air like a sweet promise.

Later, the city embraced the night, a blanket of darkness gently covering everything while vibrant lights danced across the windows of a sleek limousine. Max stood outside, holding the door open for Latoya. The chauffeur, impeccably dressed in a black suit, stood patiently nearby, his demeanor serious.

Once inside, the driver closed the door, and the limousine glided smoothly through the streets. Inside, the hum of the road provided a comforting backdrop. Max leaned closer, a mix of hope and nervousness flashing in his eyes as he fidgeted with his seatbelt.

"Latoya," he began, his voice filled with anticipation. "I've been thinking about us. Tonight feels different, and I need to say something."

"What is it?"

Gathering his courage, Max continued, "I would like to continue dating you."

"I guess it will be okay."

"Great!" Max exclaimed, a smile lighting up his face.

In that joyful moment, he reached for her hand, locking eyes with Latoya as an electric connection sparked between them. They arrived at the Florida Theater, and music flowed from the entrance, creating an atmosphere alive with energy. Max stepped out first, then moved quickly to help

Latoya exit the limousine. Hand in hand, they danced their way into the theater, laughter bursting from their lips like bubbles of joy.

Inside, the concert hall buzzed with excitement, a vibrant mix of sharp suits and casual outfits woven into a

colorful tapestry. The lights dimmed, the room quieted, anticipation hanging thick in the air as the first notes filled the space.

Max and Latoya danced and sang together, lost in the moment's magic. Leaning closer to her, Max whispered, "Latoya, I want you to know that you can trust me. If I have to apologize once, I will apologize over and over again until you believe me." Latoya inhaled deeply, processing his sincerity.

"Max, all of this is happening so fast," she said, a hint of concern in her voice. But Max's smile was reassuring, and as he edged closer, his heart began to race. The night drew to an end when their lips were on the verge of meeting, when the music swelled around them, wrapping them in a bubble of warmth and intimacy.

Latoya arrives home and goes inside. She flipped on the lights and nearly gasped when she spotted Denise asleep on the couch. She tiptoed over, trying not to wake her friend. Just as she got close, Denise stirred, stretching and opening her eyes.

"Wow, you're glowing!" Denise exclaimed, a teasing smile spreading across her face. "Either that date was amazing, or you found a hundred bucks on the sidewalk."

Latoya couldn't help but grin as memories of the night came rushing back.

"It was incredible! Once I got past the shock, I really had a great time."

"Shock?" Denise sat up, her curiosity piqued.

"Yeah! Max totally surprised me. I think I might be in love," Latoya confessed, a giddy feeling swelling in her chest. Denise shot up from the couch, her eyes wide with disbelief.

"Wait, did you just say you're in love? With Max?"

"I did!" Latoya's smile widened even more. "Denise, it just feels so different this time."

"What about online dating?" Denise asked, a hint of concern creeping in. "You know, to find the right guy?"

Latoya moved to the kitchen and opened the fridge, grabbing a Coke. Denise followed her, plopping down in a chair at the counter and snagging an apple from the fruit bowl.

"I don't think I need that dating site anymore," Latoya said, taking a sip of her soda. The bubbles made her feel even more excited. Denise arched an eyebrow.

"What about that one thing you've always said you wouldn't compromise on?" Latoya set the Coke can down, her expression turning thoughtful.

"Max has really changed, and it's for the better."

"What does he think about having kids?"

"Well, this was our first date," Latoya clarified, her voice steady. "But he did ask me for a second chance."

Denise's eyes practically popped out.

"And what did you say?"


"I told him I'd think about it," Latoya replied, a mix of excitement and uncertainty dancing in her tone.

Denise stood up, moving the blanket aside as she searched for her keys. After finding them, she headed toward the door, with Latoya following closely behind. "Okay, now that I know you're safe, I'm headed home. They walked to the front door and shared a warm hug. "Thanks, Denise, for everything."

"You know I've always got your back," Denise said, giving her one last squeeze.

# Chapter 6

The cellphone rang incessantly, drowning out the grumbling voices of frustrated customers filling the baggage service office. Latoya deftly weaved her way through the crowd; her expression remained focused despite the chaos. She reached for the paging phone and announced, "Attention, everyone! All bags for Herself Airline customers will be placed on carousel one."

Just then, Max appeared, a striking figure in his blue pilot uniform. He strode in confidently, rolling his pilot bag behind him and holding a bouquet of thirty-six purple and white roses. Latoya caught his eye as he made his way toward her.

"Latoya, I wanted to brighten up your day," Max said, halting in front of her. Latoya's eyes sparkled with surprise.

"Wow! Max, what's the occasion?"

"—I've been waiting for my luggage for half an hour!"

Latoya's demeanor shifted instantly as she turned her attention to the frustrated customer, but she couldn't completely ignore Max.

"I understand your concern. Look, your luggage is coming out now on the carousel," she reassured the woman. Max, sensing the urgency, quickly offered, "Latoya, I can help with the bags!"

"Thanks, Max, I appreciate it," she replied, grateful for his support.

Max left the office, and Latoya held the bouquet of roses close to her chest, taking a moment to enjoy the lovely surprise. At carousel number 1, bags circled slowly. Max busily pulled bags off the conveyor, assisting anxious passengers one by one.

Back in the office, Latoya was at her desk, working on her computer. The frustrated customer stood right in front of her monitor while squirming kids darted between their parents. The phone continued to ring. Latoya leaned over the keyboard, searching for answers.

"Please, everyone, your bags are not lost. Some bags were put on another flight that will arrive later today," she explained, her voice steady and calm.
Max re-entered the office, balancing the last bag from the carousel in his arms.

"The carousel is clear," he announced, relief evident in his voice.

"Thank you," Latoya replied, feeling a wave of relief wash over her. She began taking customer reports. One by one, the customers started to leave the office. She inhaled the sweet scent of her roses, and a warm smile crept across her face. Max hesitated for a moment, his gaze lingering on her as he reached out and gently took her hand. Leaning in, he pressed a soft kiss to her lips.

"Not at work — besides, cameras are everywhere," Latoya turned her head, playfully scolding him. Max flashed a mischievous grin.

"Good. Let them see. Anyway, I have to go. The plane can't fly itself."

Latoya released his hand, a bittersweet feeling tugging at her heart.

"Have a safe flight," she said as he tightened his grip around the rim of his pilot hat and moved toward the door. He glanced back one last time and caught Latoya smelling the roses, his smile widening before he hurried away.

In the busy airport public area, crowds buzzed like bees. Carmen smiled at Max as they passed each other. She entered the baggage service office, where she found Latoya sitting at her desk, still mesmerized by the bouquet in front of her. The petals twisted between her fingers, and she rearranged the blooms absentmindedly.

"More roses?" Carmen teased, raising an eyebrow. Latoya beamed at her friend.

"Uhm, Max surprised me with them." Carmen leaned over the counter, her fingers lightly touching the delicate flowers.

"Impressive. Purple and white long-stem roses. Deep admiration and a new beginning for the long term."

Latoya chuckled softly. "I've been told that before." Suddenly, the sounds of another flight arriving filled the air. The bag belts started up with a clatter, horns blowing, and the noise rose to a cacophony. Latoya hoped the reports she collected earlier would finally bear fruit.

"Ladies and gentlemen, baggage for Herself Airlines is on carousel 1," she announced into the microphone. She picked up the office keys, and she and Carmen exited the office, ready to tackle the next wave of passengers gathered around the baggage carousel number 1. Carmen leaned forward, her eyes sparkling with curiosity.

"Alright, spill the beans. And don't leave out the good parts," she urged.

Latoya paused in her frantic packing of bags; she needed a moment to gather her thoughts. Grasping Carmen's hands, she began her story, a nervous energy bubbling within her.

"So, I sat at a reserved, cozy table in the restaurant, and oh, I was so nervous!" Latoya confessed.
"I can imagine," she replied.

"Then we moved to the rooftop, and honestly, the romantic ambiance took my breath away. And get this, there were thirty-six long-stemmed red, purple, and white roses on the table! The lights were dim and soft, and the music played gently in the background."

"Wow!" Carmen exclaimed. "I can only imagine how surprised you were."

Latoya sighed happily. "Everything was perfect." Carmen beamed at her friend.

"I'm so happy for you! I know you said you weren't open to love before."

"I know," Latoya replied, her expression serious.

"But something felt right about this time." Carmen leaned in closer. "I have one more thing to say, please pray. Don't decide anything until you get an answer from God."

"I will. I promise."

The airport intercom system crackled to life, calling for customer service agent Carmen Perez to return to the airline's ticket counter.

Then, Max, standing in the airport security line, travelers adorned in flag-themed apparel swarmed around, their laughter filling the air as children waved miniature flags, darting about in excitement.

The unmistakable scent of barbecued food wafted in from the nearby restaurants. Amidst the atmosphere of camaraderie and joy, Max pulled out his phone and dialed Timothy's number.

"Hello?"

"Hey, Tim! It's Max. I got a proposal for you."

"Okay, what is it?" Timothy responded, intrigued.

"I need your help to plan a romantic trip to
Aruba."

"Absolutely! I assume your date went well."

Max chuckled, excitement bubbling within him, "I'm
thrilled to tell you how excited I am. But I'm at the airport
on my way to Vegas for an overnight trip. I'll call you when
I get back."

"Sounds like a plan," Timothy said before they ended
the call.

Max walked through security; his mind wandered to the
possibilities awaiting him.

Later on that night, Latoya sat at her desk, absorbed in
a wave of emails. The flickering screen illuminated her face
as she sifted through the messages. Then an unexpected
title caught her eye: 'Customer Service Agent of the
Quarter.'

She read the details, and her heart raced with joy. A two-
week vacation package to the Brickell Bay Beach Club and
Spa in Aruba was the prize. A wide smile spread across her
face, and she could hardly believe her luck. Without
hesitating, she grabbed her phone and dialed Denise's
number.

"Hello?"

"Denise, it's me, Latoya! I won the Customer Service Agent for the Quarter award!" Latoya exclaimed, her excitement bubbling over.

"I know — it was posted on the notice board in the break room. Congrats!" Denise responded, happiness clear in her voice.

"I can't believe I won a two-night Aruba vacation package!"

"Take me! — wait — are you taking Max?"

Latoya's mind raced, "What do you think? Should I ask him? Do you think he will want to go?" she questioned, uncertainty creeping in."

"Uhm, you should be careful — I don't want you to get hurt again by Max," Denise cautioned.

Latoya shook her head, her resolve strengthening at her friend's concern, "No, I don't think he wants to hurt me. I will ask him. When you talk to Carmen, please share the good news and ask her to call me." "Okay, just be careful," Denise urged.

Latoya hung up, her thoughts still racing. She stared hard at her phone for a moment, considering her next move. Finally, she picked up the phone again and dialed Max's number. After several rings, there was no answer.

"Hi Max, this is Latoya. Please call me when you get this message," she left in a warm tone, hoping he would respond. Taking a deep breath, she locked the office and then, I headed to lunch, heart buzzing with both excitement and uncertainty.

At Denise's house, she sat on her bed, leaning back against the plush pillows that comforted her weary body. After hanging up the phone, a peaceful sense washed over her as she brushed her hand gently across her stomach in a soothing motion. An unspoken bond was forming, filled with warmth and hope.

"How are you doing in there, my sweet baby?" she whispered, her voice barely audible, as if the words were a lullaby meant for the life within her.

With a satisfied sigh and a flutter of affection, she fluffed her pillow and settled her head down, the quiet of the night wrapping around her like a comforting blanket. Closing her eyes, she allowed herself to drift, thoughts of Latoya's celebration mingling with her own dreams for the future.

Max had just come home from an overnight trip, trudging through the familiar rooms of his house with an unsettling feeling nagging at him. The echo of his footsteps filled the silence, and he absentmindedly checked his messages.

In a distracted moment, he tripped over a shoe left carelessly on the floor. Frustration welled up inside him, but it quickly faded as he noticed a missed call from Latoya. A surge of eager anticipation filled him as he dialed her number, his heart pounding in rhythm with his thoughts.

"Hello, I'm not available. Please leave a message," Latoya's voice came through the speaker. It was warm and inviting— just the tone he longed to hear live.

"Hey, Latoya! It's Max. I'm so sorry I missed your call! I was thirty thousand feet in the air. Please call me back!" he recorded, urgency and regret threading through his voice. What could Latoya have wanted?

His mind raced with possibilities. Max decided to reach out to his confidante, Denise. He dialed her number, the phone pressed to his ear as he paced the floor, hope flickering within him.

"Hello."

"Denise, it's Max. Do you have a minute?" he asked when she answered, trying to keep his tone steady.

"Sure—what's up?"

"I need your help—again—to pull off the best date in history," he said, a hint of desperation creeping into his words.

"Sorry, Max—I can't help you anymore. I've gotten you to this point; now you're on your own," she said, a finality laced in her tone.

His heart sank. "Wait, did I do something wrong?"

"No, nothing's wrong. You can handle everything from here. Besides, Latoya is my friend, and I can't bear the thought of her getting hurt again."

"Wait a second, who said anything about hurting Latoya? Of all people, you know I would never hurt her again," Max replied, a nervous energy taking over as he stood. "Denise, you do know that you are the reason I've gotten this far with Latoya. I promise you, I will never hurt her," he insisted.

"Not intentionally," Denise replied, her words hanging between them like an unwelcome shadow. "What does that mean?" he pressed, confused.

"Nothing. Forget what I said. I can't help anymore. You're on your own," Denise stated firmly before hanging up. While staring at the phone in disbelief, Max felt the weight of the conversation pressing down on him. He sank onto the edge of his bed, his head bowed as uncertainty enveloped him.

Later that night, as Latoya drove down the quiet streets, a sense of accomplishment mingled with the evening's calm. She reached for her phone and spotted a missed call from Max.

Curiosity piqued, she quickly dialed his number, the excitement fluttering in her chest.

"Hello."

"Max, it's Latoya. You called?" she replied, trying to suppress the thrill bubbling within her.

Max hesitated, his heart racing. "Uh, yes, I did call. I was returning your call."

Latoya could feel the tension dissolve as her enthusiasm burst forth. "Oh, I did call earlier today.  I wanted to share my good news!"

"What is it? Tell me!"

"I won Employee of the Quarter, and the prize is a four-day, three-night hotel vacation package for two in Aruba!"

"Vacation in Aruba? Really?" Max exclaimed, bouncing off his bed and rushing to his computer, inspiration igniting in his mind. "You're not going to believe this, but I traded my shifts for an overnight trip in Aruba in two months. Who are you taking with you?"

"That's why I was calling—but it seems you already have plans.

"No—I mean—I was going to invite you to come to Aruba with me—only as friends. Nothing disrespectful," he blurted out, his heart racing with hopeful admiration.

"You were?" Latoya asked, surprise coloring her voice.

"Yes! When can you use your prize?" Max inquired, eager to make their plans official.

"Anytime, but I have to book the trip within the next thirty days."

"Okay. I'll book flight 5683. You can also book your flight if that's your preference. Let's make it a date."

"Okay. It's a date."

Latoya turned up the radio as she drove home, her heart humming with dreams of the future. She pulled into her driveway, her headlights casting a warm glow along the path. A wave of anticipation washed over her as she reached for the vacation package resting in the passenger seat. With a key in hand, she stepped out of the car and made her way to the front door, excitement fluttering into her chest. Once inside her house, Latoya dropped her keys onto the kitchen table, the sound echoing in the stillness of the night. There was no time to waste. She hurried to her computer desk, her fingers already itching to book her dream getaway.

Flopping into the comfy chair, she fired up her laptop, buzzing with excitement as she dove into booking her flight to Aruba. With each click, she felt the city hustle fade away, replaced by visions of sun-soaked beaches and vibrant nightlife.

She scrolled through hotel options, her fingers flying across the keys, imagining herself sipping cocktails in the sand and soaking up the sun. This trip was going to be epic!

"Alexia, please play some jazz music."

Settling back in the chair, the day's fatigue caught up with her. Latoya closed her eyes, allowing herself to drift off to the soothing sounds of jazz.

* * *

Two months later, Max found himself at the breakfast table in his tidy home, the sunlight streaming in through the window. The kitchen, filled with modern appliances and organized wooden cabinets overflowing with dishes and aviation-themed cookbooks, radiated a sense of calm.

As he munched on a banana, his attention was drawn to the weather channel flickering on the television. Suddenly, a determined look crossed his face. He picked up his phone, dialed Timothy's number, and waited.

"Hello."

"Tim, it's Max. Change of plans."

"Okay, tell me what's wrong?"

"Nothing's wrong," Max assured him, taking a deep breath, "but you might think I'm a little crazy. You know, I was planning to propose to Latoya on the trip to Aruba."

"Uhm…marriage proposal?"

Max's heart raced as he forged ahead. "I've made a firm decision. I'm not just proposing; I'm taking charge of the whole wedding planning process." A laugh broke the tension on Timothy's end.

"You've caught me off guard. I never saw this coming. Max, are you serious?"

"Yes, I am," Max insisted, the resolve in his voice shining through. "Man, I'm not the one in control here. This is a divine plan orchestrated by my God."

With every word, Max's conviction grew. He felt it was a golden opportunity he couldn't let slip away.

"Tim, you don't know this, but Latoya has always wanted to visit Aruba. Do I think it's a coincidence that she won a trip to Aruba? No, I believe it's divine intervention."

"Wow! That's beautiful, man," Timothy responded. "Alright, so you want to get engaged and have a wedding ceremony in Aruba? Let's do it. Do you have a ring yet? Who's going to officiate?" Max took a steady breath, feeling the weight of his choices.

"This is where you come in as a Minister. Please understand how important this is to me; it would mean everything if you officiated my wedding. Your friendship is everything. And I really could use your help in picking out Latoya's ring, something that encapsulates my love and commitment to her."

"It would be my honor to help you create a wedding that transcends the ordinary into a sacred celebration filled with love and spiritual beauty." "Thank you so much, Tim.

"I'm free tomorrow, so let's go ring shopping, Tim offers as he hangs up.

# Chapter 7

Tuesday morning had dawned bright and promising at the ticket counter. Carmen and Denise were busy chatting with passengers, their friendly smiles making everyone feel at ease. Then, Latoya approached the counter, looking both determined and a little anxious

"Hey, can I ask you a favor?" she said, almost breathless. "Can someone check my mail while I'm away? This trip means a lot to me, but I'm really not sure what to expect when I get back." Denise perked up immediately.

"Absolutely! I'd be happy to help. Is Max going with you?" Latoya nodded, a small gesture that said so much.

"Yeah," she whispered, glancing down for a moment.

"But I told him I'm scared of being vulnerable again. Still, I really want to give this a shot." Carmen jumped in, her smile warm and encouraging.

"That's awesome! Go have an amazing time; you deserve it." Latoya felt the weight lift slightly as she turned to leave.

Excitement bubbled up inside her, mixed with a hint of anxiety. Denise called after her.

"Seriously, have the best time!" "Thanks, you two!" Latoya replied, her heart racing as she stepped away from the counter and toward her adventure. Once on the plane, Latoya squeezed into her seat in the middle section. The vibe in the air buzzed with anticipation, and her head swam with thoughts about what lay ahead.

It felt electric.

In the cockpit, Max sat next to Timothy, trying to steady his nerves. He gripped the armrest, feeling the weight of everything they had planned together.

"Hey, man, how's it going?" Timothy asked, shooting Max a supportive smile.

"Honestly? Shaking in my boots here," Max laughed nervously. "I can't believe I'm actually doing this. What if she says no? What if I'm not enough for her?" Timothy chuckled lightly and placed a hand on Max's shoulder.

"C'mon, you've got this! Did you write down everything you wanted to say?"

"I did," Max said, a flicker of disbelief crossing his face. "But still…"

"Don't overthink it. She's formidable, and you're awesome. Just be yourself," Timothy reassured him. "And remember, you're a pilot; you're in control of this landing. So make it a smooth one."

As the last few passengers boarded, including Latoya, Max's heart rate accelerated. The cabin doors closed behind them, sealing their fates together as the plane prepared for takeoff. It was happening.

In the cabin, the atmosphere buzzed with the chatter and laughter of eager travelers, all heading to Aruba. The sun streamed through the small windows, warming the faces of passengers who chatted excitedly or flipped through magazines. At the front of the cabin, a young flight attendant stood poised, her warm voice cutting through the noise.

"Good morning, ladies and gentlemen. On behalf of the crew, I'd like to welcome you aboard flight 5683, non-stop service to Aruba. We have been cleared for takeoff." Her reassuring tone set the stage for what was to come.

As the plane ascended into the bright blue sky, the passengers settled into their seats. Some read, while others continued their conversations, visions of vacation dancing in their minds.

Then, a momentary jolt of turbulence broke the calm that had enveloped the cabin. The Captain's voice came over the intercom, cutting through the chatter, commanding attention.

"This is your Captain speaking. I need Latoya Marino to ring her call button so the flight attendant can identify her."

Latoya sat quietly, her fingers nervously fiddling with her eyeglasses. As the Captain's voice echoed again, she felt her heart quicken.

"Is there a Latoya Marino onboard? Please raise your hand so that the flight attendant can identify you." Hesitation washed over her. She tapped her fingers on the armrest, weighing her options, before summoning the courage to press the call button. A moment later, the flight attendant appeared at her side, a curious expression on her face.

"Latoya, please get up and come with me," she said gently, guiding her into the aisle.

Confused and surprised, Latoya gripped the seats for support as she made her way forward. At the front of the plane, a familiar figure knelt, revealing a small velvet box. It was Max. His eyes sparkled under the cabin lights, matching the glimmer of the engagement ring nestled inside the box. Gasps filled the cabin as whispers of excitement rippled through the crowd.

"Latoya," Max began, his voice steady yet filled with emotion, "I know you said you're scared of being vulnerable, but I also know you said you'd try for us." Latoya's breath hitched in her throat, tears brimming in her eyes. Her heart raced—a mixture of fear and hope swirling inside her. She stumbled slightly, reaching for Max's steady hand to steady herself.

The passengers exchanged supportive glances, the tension in the air transforming into encouragement.

"If we leave our past behind and embrace what's ahead," Max continued, locking his gaze onto hers,

"I promise you'll never regret this."

Latoya felt herself wavering as his words struck a chord deep within her. She gripped the top of a nearby passenger's seat, trying to steady herself amidst the whirlwind of her emotions.

"Let me be your one and only. I vow to love you fiercely. Latoya, will you marry me?"

"Say Yes! Say Yes!"—the supportive voices merging into a joyful flood. Max stepped closer, his expression earnest,

"Please, Latoya, will you marry me?"

"I love you, Max. But... I've been hurt before, and I'm scared. I'm not sure if I'm ready. But I want to give it a try... Yes! Yes! I will marry you."

A sudden jolt of turbulence rocked the plane, landing Latoya right into Max's arms.

It was magical as he slipped the ring onto her finger, sealing their new reality. Their lips met in a kiss, intoxicating and sweet, celebrated by cheers and applause from the surrounding passengers.

"I've dreamed of this moment for so long," Max confessed, his voice thick with emotion. "I'm incredibly blessed and grateful. Latoya, you've made me the happiest man alive. I love you more than words can say."

As he embraced her, joy radiated through the cabin. After their moment, Max returned to the cockpit, leaving Timothy, the co-pilot, to address the crowd.

"Congratulations! Latoya and Max!" Timothy called, his excitement infectious. Latoya gazed down at her ring; a radiant symbol of love and dreams shared a promise of the beautiful journey ahead.

"Look at this breathtaking ring," Timothy said, lifting her hand for everyone to see. "It's a shimmering testament to love, commitment, and the promise of forever. This is one of the most romantic proposals I've ever witnessed. My boy truly captured the essence of love in this moment."

Returning to the cockpit, Timothy exchanged knowing smiles with Max, who was still riding high from the proposal.

"Thanks, man, for that heartfelt toast. You know what's next."

"Yes, I do..." Timothy replied, aware of the weight behind those hopeful words.

"They're the words I pray to hear Latoya say," Max said softly.

"Amen, brother. Amen."

Timothy headed back out to join in the celebration, raising a glass to toast the newly engaged couple.

"One more toast to Max and Latoya!" he called, echoing a celebration that would resonate long after the flight landed. And above the clouds, amidst the cheers and laughter, a new chapter began for Max and Latoya, one filled with promise and love.

"I can't wait to tell my mom and dad, Denise, and Carmen. I really hope they're happy for me," Latoya said, her heart practically bursting with excitement.

"I'm sure they will be," Timothy said, trying to reassure her.

As the plane began to descend, the flight attendant's voice came over the cabin again, instructing everyone to prepare for landing. You could feel the joy and excitement in the air, mixed with the thrill of new beginnings and adventures waiting just beyond the clouds. Then, the flight attendant spoke into the mic, her voice calm and clear.

"We're experiencing some congestion on the tarmac, so air traffic control has put us on a ten-minute hold. Please stay seated until the Captain turns off the seatbelt sign."

Someone in the back piped up, adding a dash of humor to the situation. "In that case, may we all have more champagne?"

"Absolutely! Champagne for everyone!" the flight attendant replied with enthusiasm. The cabin filled with laughter as passengers raised their glasses in anticipation.

After what felt like an eternity of waiting, the attendant announced cheerfully.

"We've been cleared to exit the plane. Once you've disembarked from the plane, please collect your baggage from the carousel. Welcome to Aruba!"

As everyone disembarked, a chorus of Congratulatory remarks erupted around Latoya and Max.

"Congratulations, Latoya and Max, on your engagement!" Stepping outside onto the tarmac, Latoya felt the sun shining down, casting a warm glow.

The runway was scattered with lovely purple and white rose petals. Palm trees waved gently, and vibrant buildings danced along with the sweet melody of

"Here Comes the Bride" is playing softly in the background. Latoya's heart soared as she held Timothy's arm, excitement lighting up her face. In the crowd, her parents stood waiting, her mom with her gorgeous salt-and-pepper hair and her dad looking sharp in a three-piece suit.

"What are you doing here?" she exclaimed, surprised to see them.

"We were invited," her parents said in unison, smiles stretching across their faces. Latoya's eyes sparkled as she shared her big news.

"Can you believe it? I'm engaged!"

Just then, Max revealed his surprise: a beautiful, intimate wedding ceremony set up right there on the tarmac, surrounded by Latoya's parents and flight crew.

As the music shifted, everyone took their places. Timothy took his place beside Latoya, acting as the officiant. Her dad took her hand and guided her down the aisle, emotions flooding over her.

"Wait, what's going on?" Latoya asked, her brow knitting in confusion.

"You're getting married—that's why we're all here," her dad said with a gentle smile. Tears began to stream down Latoya's cheeks as realization hit her.

She looked from her parents to Max, feeling the weight of the moment settle in her heart. This was really her wedding.  In a whisper to herself, Latoya thought, 'I never thought I'd get here… but here I am, choosing to trust again. I do. I'll love you, Max, always.' Timothy's voice filled the air as he started the ceremony,

"Dearly beloved, we have gathered here today, in the sight of God, to join this man and this woman in holy matrimony. If anyone has reason why these two should not be married, let them speak now or forever hold their peace."

He paused and then continued, "Who gives this woman to be joined in marriage with this man?" Latoya's parents replied together.

"We do."

"Maximus Jones, do you take Latoya Marino to be your wedded wife, to live together in holy matrimony, to forsake all others, and keep yourself only unto her for as long as you both live?" "I do," Max said confidently.

"Latoya Marino, do you take Maximus Jones as your wedded husband, to live together in holy matrimony, to forsake all others, and keep yourself unto him for as long as you live?" Her voice trembles, Latoya whispered.

"I do." Love filled the atmosphere; it was infectious.

"Now, the rings, please," Timothy instructed, his voice steady. Max held the ring in his palm, its glimmer highlighting the love around them.

"Do you, Max, give this ring to Latoya as a token of your love for her?" Timothy asked, watching the couple share a silent promise in their gaze. With a warm smile, Max carefully placed the ring on Latoya's finger.

"I do."

Timothy then turned to Latoya.

"Do you, Latoya, give this ring to Max as a token of your love for him?" With a shaky yet determined voice, Latoya responded.

"I've never been surer of anything in my life, Max, you're my forever." Timothy turned back to Max.

"Will you wear this ring as evidence of your love for Latoya?"

"Yes—and you're mine, Latoya, forever and always," Max replied, his voice full of promise.

Timothy smiled warmly at the couple, sensing the sincerity of their vows.

"By the power vested in me, I now pronounce you husband and wife. You may kiss the bride."

Max leaned in, his eyes sparkling with happiness. Latoya met him halfway, and in that sweet moment, they shared a tender kiss that ignited cheers and applause from their loved ones.

The warmth of their affection enveloped the tarmac as they embraced, the world around them fading away. They stepped back, hand in hand, beaming at each other. The cheering crowd surrounded them, showering them with well-wishes.

Latoya could hardly believe how everything had unfolded—one moment, she was celebrating her engagement, and the next, she was married to Max. As they made their way down the aisle, her parents joined them, wrapping her in a loving embrace.

"Congratulazioni! Tanti auguri per il vostro matrimonio," her mom said, wiping away happy tears.

"Grazie, mamma e papa," I never imagined this would happen today," Latoya replied, still in disbelief.

"But I wouldn't trade it for anything." Max chuckled, his arm pulling her closer.

"Neither would I. You surprised me completely. I thought we were celebrating our engagement!"

Latoya laughed, the joy bubbling up inside her. "Well, I guess we can say it became a double celebration!"

As they posed for pictures, smiles illuminated their faces, and the presence of the crew and family felt perfect. They shared light-hearted jokes and reminisced about their journey together, each moment solidifying the bond they had formed.

As the sun began to set, casting a golden glow over the tarmac, Latoya and Max found a quiet corner away from the crowd. Latoya rested her head on Max's shoulder, feeling content.

"Can you believe we're actually married?" she asked, blushing slightly. Max chuckled again, looking down at her.

"Honestly? No. But I wouldn't want to be anywhere else right now. You have made me the happiest man alive." Latoya smiled back, feeling a warmth spread through her chest.

"And you've taught me to believe in love again. It feels incredible." Max squeezed her hand, the meaning behind their smiles deepening.

"We're just getting started, Latoya. Whatever comes next, we'll face it together."

# Chapter 8

The air buzzed with excitement as night fell over Jacksonville Airport. Friends and family filled the rows of chairs, anticipation palpable in the atmosphere. Flight 36 had just landed from Aruba, bringing a wave of eager travelers. Among them, Latoya and Max stepped off the plane, their faces glowing with joy.

As Latoya spotted her friends, Denise, and Carmen, she lit up, her voice ringing out. "Hey, guys!"

"Latoya! How was your vacation?" Denise and Carmen replied in unison, their eagerness unmistakable. Latoya's smile grew wider.

"You won't believe what happened in Aruba!" Denise leaned in, her brow furrowed with curiosity. "Tell me… what went wrong?" Max, standing close by, offered Denise a reassuring smile. He pulled Latoya close, their connection clear to anyone who watched.

"Nothing went wrong. Everything went right," they declared in harmony. However, Denise's narrowed eyes hinted at some skepticism.

"It's the way you said, 'you are not going to believe what happened in Aruba.' It sounded... disappointing." Latoya shook her head, resolute.

"No disappointment—not even close. In fact, I'm inviting my best friends to the dinner party, Max and I am hosting at Ponte Vedra Inn and Club this Saturday at 6 p.m."

Denise's eyes sparkled with excitement. "Absolutely, I'll be there!"

"Ditto," Carmen added.

Latoya subtly concealed her ring finger while extending her hand. Carmen handed her a piece of mail. Max intertwined his fingers with Latoya's, a tender gesture, and they walked away together, leaving Denise and Carmen to ponder the implications of Latoya's invitation.

Inside the employee checkout room, a soft tick-tock of a time clock echoed against the walls adorned with lockers and lunch tables. Denise and Carmen hurriedly gathered their belongings; urgency filled their movements.

"Denise, why did you immediately assume that something went wrong for Latoya in Aruba?" Carmen asked, her tone laced with confusion.

Denise shrugged, her expression turning serious.

"A dinner party… do you think she's pregnant?"

Carmen's eyes widened in disbelief.

"What? No! That's your life. I'm thinking about an engagement announcement."

"Engagement? No way, they just met," Denise countered, shaking her head.

"Actually, they just re-met. They were married before. I tell you, Denise, it wouldn't surprise me if they did get engaged," Carmen insisted passionately. Denise punched in her sign-out code, unease hanging in the air.

"We'll just have to wait and see." As they exited the break room, chatter about the upcoming dinner party filled their thoughts.

Morning dawned bright at the Ponte Vedra Inn and Club, where a wall-to-wall television buzzed with activity. Two large chandeliers hung elegantly over a bridal table draped in white and purple, creating an inviting atmosphere.

Max and his friend Timothy sat together at a breakfast table, fine-tuning the menu and making seating arrangements for the upcoming Saturday dinner party.

"Max, your love story has inspired me to tell Denise... to confess my love for her," Timothy said, determination settling into his voice. Max sipped his coffee, contemplating Timothy's admission.

"If you love her, man, just tell her."

Latoya's parents arrived, and warm greetings were exchanged with Max.

"Good morning, young men. Max, I'm having a blast," Mr. Marino said, patting him affectionately.

"Yes, and I'm more excited about tomorrow night," Latoya's mom added, settling beside her husband. As Timothy stood to leave, he looked at Max earnestly.

"It's something to be excited about. Max, man, I'll see you later."

"Sure. And again, thank you." Max rose to hug Timothy, grateful for his support. Latoya's parents bid him farewell as Timothy departed.

"Mom, Dad, I wish you a good breakfast! Enjoy all the amenities here. I'll see you both tomorrow night," Max said, anticipation bubbling within him for the events ahead.

* * *

Max arrived at Latoya's house, where two black travel bags lay on the bed. Clothing was scattered across the surface, and boxes of ladies' shoes cluttered the floor. Latoya sat beside Max on the floor, deep in thought as she tried to decide what to pack. "What should I pack?" she asked, her brow furrowing with concern.

"Nothing, you are all I need," Max chuckled, trying to lighten the mood.

"Max, I'm serious."

"I'm serious too. I get it, you don't understand yet, but eventually you will." Max knelt; his gaze fixed on Latoya as he recalled his earnest plea to God for a second chance at their love.

In a moment of vulnerability, he had made a promise that if granted another opportunity, he would never take it for granted again. Latoya looked at him, caught off guard by the depth of his sincerity.

Max's heart raced at the thought of the journey ahead, filled with hope and determination. He turned his gaze to Latoya. He was struck by the tears shimmering in her eyes, a reflection of the tempest swirling within her heart.

In an instinctive gesture that spoke volumes, she reached for his hand, her fingers intertwining with his, seeking the comfort and connection only he could give. With a newfound determination, Max continued,

"Now I will honor my promise to God and to you."

His voice held a gravity that underscored every word, binding them together with threads of unwavering faith and love. Latoya sat at the edge of the bed, a soft smile blossoming on her lips as her affection illuminated her eyes.

"I love you too, Max," she whispered, her gaze filled with warmth.

"Then let's go do it," he replied, a playful grin spreading across his face, revealing the joy that surged within him. Together, they worked to pack their bags, a choreography of shared purpose.

Latoya, with her dainty suitcase and purse, and Max, effortlessly managing the larger ones. Once they were loaded into the car, excitement tingled in the air, wrapping around them like an embrace.

An hour later, they arrived at the Ponte Vedra Inn and Club, the hotel's majestic architecture enveloping them in an enchanting allure. The beautiful stretch of beach, lined with swaying palms and manicured lawns, promised serenity as waves danced playfully upon the shore.

In the parking lot, their friend Timothy burst into their view, energetically running in circles and exclaiming, "I love her, I love her, I love Denise!"

His exuberance, mixed with his evident intoxication, provided comedic relief amidst the intimate tension.

"Did he just say he loves Denise?" Latoya furrowed her brow, concern mingling with disbelief.

"Yep, he's definitely drunk," Max chuckled as he opened the trunk to retrieve their suitcases.

"I'll talk to him. You, my darling, can go settle into our room." Latoya shook her head, a bittersweet smile flitting across her lips.

"You know what's sad? Denise doesn't want anything to do with him." With a gentle squeeze of Max's hand, she took her bags and walked toward their room, leaving him to manage the situation with Timothy. Max approached his friend, slinging Timothy's arm over his shoulder, their friendship shining through even in this moment of chaos.

"Okay, buddy. Let's get you to your room. Remember, we have a big day tomorrow."

Inside the Ponte Vedra Inn, the foyer unfolded with lavish beauty, but Timothy's state contrasted starkly with the opulence surrounding them. Stumbling forward, tears streamed down his cheeks as he cried out, "I love her, man. And I love you, Max."

"I know," Max replied, sincerity lacing his voice as he ushered Timothy into their room. "Get some sleep."

In the small bathroom, Timothy gripped the edge of the sink as panic washed over him, vulnerability bared in the reflection staring back at him.

"Never again, never again," he murmured, resting his forehead against the cool porcelain, seeking relief from the tempest within.

"Now that you've emptied yourself, get up off the floor," Max said, his tone a blend of firmness and compassion. He helped Timothy into bed, removed his shoes, and gently turned off the lights before slipping

quietly out of the room. The weight of the evening hung heavily on both friends, their paths diverging yet ever intertwined in their struggles.

It's the morning of the wedding party, in the bustling expanse of the airport, where announcements echo through the high ceilings, mingling with the muffled chatter and the rumble of luggage being wheeled across the polished floors.

A long line of weary travelers snaked its way toward the check-in counters, their faces showing the strain of travel. Some fidgeted impatiently, stealing glances at their watches, while others stared blankly ahead, glued to the glow of their phones.

Carmen, standing behind the ticket counter, felt a wave of relief washing over her as she checked in the last passenger. The incessant noise of the airport—announcements, rolling suitcases, and chattering travelers—began to fade slightly as she stepped away from the bustling counter. With a quiet sigh, she reached for her phone, dialing Denise's number, her fingers dancing over the familiar buttons as she thought of her friend.

As the phone rang, she could almost picture Denise's tousled hair and sleepy eyes.

"Denise," she said after a few rings, her voice cutting through the background chatter like a beacon, bringing calm amid the chaos.

From the other end, Denise's voice floated back, thick with sleep.

"Oh, my God! I'm so sorry, I totally overslept— I'm on my way!" The panic in her tone made Carmen smile; she could envision her friend scrambling to get ready, probably throwing on mismatched socks and her favorite hoodie.

"Hey, no worries at all," Carmen reassured her, warmth flooding her voice. "It's three of us here, and honestly, it's Saturday—a pretty slow day. You should sleep in." She paused, her heart swelling with fondness for their friendship. "And don't forget to give the Supervisor a call, okay?" Carmen's words were filled with understanding.

"Thanks, Carmen! You're a lifesaver. See you tonight!" Denise replied, her relief evident even through the line, before hanging up. Carmen could almost hear the rustle of sheets as Denise likely flopped back onto her bed, grateful for the extra minutes of rest.

With a sense of anticipation for the shift ahead, Carmen tucked her phone away and dove back into her work, surrounded by the frenetic energy of the airport. It was a familiar setting, buzzing with life, and she felt invigorated as she prepared for whatever the day had in store.

Amidst the chaos, Denise nestled back into the warm cocoon of her covers, pulling them tightly over her head.

The noise of the airport felt a world away as she reveled in the unexpected opportunity to recharge.

She smiled at the thought of Latoya's and Max's dinner party later that evening, already dreaming of the laughter, good food, and the joy of reconnecting with friends. For now, though, the soft embrace of sleep beckoned, promising her the rest she desperately needed.

Morning light spilled through the curtains, casting a warm glow upon Latoya's slumbering form, nestled beneath the sheets. Oblivious to the world awakening around her, she lay cradled in sweet dreams.

Max busied himself in the kitchen, the rich aroma of hot pancakes and crispy bacon dancing through the air, mingling with the inviting scent of freshly brewed coffee. With a breakfast tray balanced in his hands, Max approached the bed, a playful glint sparkling in his eyes. Leaning in, he teased gently, It."

"Good morning! Um-hum, two sugars, one creamer."

"Just as I remembered," he replied, warmth blossoming within him as he took in her radiant beauty. "Take your time enjoying it."

After making a quick call to the front desk to ensure everything was in place for the dinner party later, Max returned to the bedroom, finding Latoya happily finishing her breakfast, the tray nearly empty.

"Wow! You devoured it."

"Let's stay here a little longer, just the two of us," her eyes dancing with mischief.

"That sounds wonderful."

They settled onto the sofa, cuddled under a cozy blanket, as the soft glow of the morning enveloped them.

# Chapter 9

P onte Vedra Inn Reception Hall was bustling as the dinner party unfolded. Max sat at the head table, directly beside Latoya. The bridesmaid took the left end of the table, while the groomsmen gathered on the right. Timothy, seated directly to Latoya's left, was buzzing with excitement. Latoya's mother sat next to Max, and her father held court at the other end.

In the corners of the room, large screens played videos of Latoya's and Max's breathtaking proposal and their recent wedding ceremony in Aruba.

"How beautiful is this?" Timothy remarked, surveying the elegantly decorated hall.

"Simply gorgeous," Latoya's mother replied, her smile spreading wide.

As the guests began to arrive, Denise walked into the hall alone. Timothy's gaze sharpened when he spotted her.

"Here comes my bride," he said, though a flicker of anxiety coursed through him.

Latoya's father turned to Timothy, his brow furrowing.

"Is that her, Denise? Timothy nodded eagerly.

"Yes, sir, that's her. Excuse me."

Denise stood next to Carmen, and Timothy wasted no time in striding over to them.

"Hello, ladies," he said, trying to exude confidence. "Denise, do you have a minute?"

"Not really. Whatever it is you need to say, say it," Denise replied, crossing her arms defensively.

Timothy took a breath.

"Okay, I'm just going to say it. Denise, I think I'm in love with you." Her reaction was sharp.

"God! No."

"God! Yes," he insisted, raising his voice slightly. "And I know you say the baby you're carrying isn't mine, but that doesn't matter." Pulling him aside, Denise's frustration was palpable.

"Timothy, I don't know how to say this any clearer. Please leave me alone! I do not love you, and you don't love me."

"Yes, Denise, I do love you," he retorted, a note of desperation creeping into his voice.

"Stop saying that," she snapped as she turned her back on him. Timothy stood there, dejected, with his head hung low. Denise joined Carmen, both drawn to the big screens, that show Max and Latoya's engagement and wedding ceremony.

"Is that Max and Latoya?" Denise asked, her brow knitting together.

"It certainly looks to be," Carmen replied, her eyes shining with curiosity.

"Are they married?"

As the night continued, the atmosphere shifted when music began, accompanied by a live wedding ceremony on the big screens. Guests filled their glasses and indulged in an extravagant feast. Max stood up, commanding the room's attention.

"May I have everyone's attention, please?" he announced, the DJ lowering the music.

"I am happy to announce that Latoya and I are married," Max declared with a proud smile. Latoya rose beside him, glass held high.

"Yes, we got married in Aruba this past weekend. We wanted to share our love with our closest family and friends." Timothy stood, holding a glass as well, his expression a mix of joy and sincerity.

"I think it's only fitting that the best man toasts the bride and groom. To Latoya and Max, I love you all, and I pray for love, peace, and all the happiness your hearts can hold." The wedding party and guests raised their glasses in unison.

"Cheers!" they called out enthusiastically.

As the DJ turned up the music, Denise slowly stood, glass in hand. The music was turned down. The room hushed, all eyes on her as she began her toast.

"I would like to make a toast to my coworker, Latoya," she said, her tone subdued. "This is not how I dreamed this would turn out for you. And to Max, my friend, and that unforgettable one-night stand we shared. To Max, my unborn baby's father!

Cheers!"

A collective gasp erupted from the crowd, disbelief hanging heavy in the air.

"Oh my God. What did she say?" Timothy exclaimed, stunned.

"Denise, what did you just say?" Max asked, confusion etched on his face. Denise raised her glass higher, her fists clenched.

"Max, you are the father of my unborn child," she declared, cutting through the silence like ice.

Loud chatter filled the room as guests whispered in shock. Latoya fell back into her chair, her face pale, while her parents rushed to console her.

"Denise, what's going on? Why are you saying that Max is the father of your unborn child?" Latoya demanded, hurt and confusion dancing in her eyes.

"It's true. Max is the father," Denise insisted, her resolve unwavering. Latoya's heart raced as questions flooded her mind. "I didn't know you were pregnant. When? How?"

"No, I can't be the father!" Max interrupted, panic rising in his voice. "This is ludicrous. It is totally impossible. Denise, I have never been with you in that way. Never!"

"Why, Denise? Why are you doing this?" Carmen pressed, concern etched across her face.

"Max needs to know. And Latoya is his wife now, so she needs to know as well," Denise stated firmly. With that, she placed her glass on the table and turned to leave the ceremony. In that moment, it felt like the ground shifted beneath them all, leaving a whirlwind of questions and tension in its wake.

Latoya felt her world spinning out of control. She pushed her chair back and grabbed her purse, leaning toward Max with urgency.

"Max, let's go," she said, her voice thick with emotion.

Max shook his head, frustration overtaking him.

"No, no, no. This is our wedding reception. I'm not leaving, and I don't want you to go either," he insisted.

Latoya's heart raced. "I'm leaving," she said firmly.

"I can't just stay here and pretend everything is fine."

"Please, Latoya, you have to trust me. I'm not the father," Max pleaded, dropping to his knees in front of her. "I'm telling you the truth. Please, we can't just leave our guests." For a moment, Latoya's expression softened, uncertainty flickering in her eyes. After a brief pause, she sighed.

"Alright, okay, I'll stay," she finally said, her voice barely above a whisper. The silence hung heavily between them as the weight of the evening pressed down. Latoya sat with her arms folded, scanning the reception hall, a slight frown creasing her brow. Max stood nearby, relief washing over him. "Thank you," he said quietly.

Timothy, the Best Man, then stood to make an announcement.

"Please, everyone," he called out, his voice rising above the soft murmur of the guests. "Max apologizes for the interruption, but he's asking that no one leave.

There's plenty of food and drinks.

Please stay and enjoy the ceremony."

It was as if a spell had been cast; the guests continued enjoying the evening, laughter and chatter mingling in the air. Later that night, outside the reception hall, some guests were leaving, while others were arriving; the atmosphere buzzed with celebration.

Max and Timothy stood off to the side, deep in conversation. "Man, this has been one eventful night," Timothy said, regret tinging his voice. "I hate to leave you, but I have a morning flight to catch."

"Yeah, I get it. Someone's got to fly the planes,"

Max replied with a chuckle, feeling a weight lift. "Tim, I really want to thank you for everything. You're the best, Best Man I could've asked for. I mean it."

"It's been my honor," Timothy said sincerely. But then he hesitated, a serious note creeping into his tone. "But I have to ask… is there any truth to what Denise said?" Max protested immediately, stepping back, his expression turning serious.

"No! I have never been with Denise like that. I know I've had my share of past relationships, but never with her." Timothy nodded slowly, studying Max's face.

"I believe you. But do you know what else? I think the baby could be mine." Max stared at him, disbelief flooding his features.

"Your baby? Really? I remember you saying you and Denise was more than friends at one point."

"I'm not sure, but it's possible," Timothy admitted, concern lacing his voice. "Listen, Max, if I were you, I would get a paternity test."

"You're right. Definitely," Max agreed, his mind racing. "Thanks again for everything." They hugged, their brotherly bond solidified by shared moments and challenges.

"It was my pleasure," Timothy said, stepping back with a smile. "Now go back to your beautiful bride, and I'll be praying for you." Max nodded, then turned to find Latoya as Timothy prepared to leave for the evening.

The next day at Herself Airlines, the atmosphere buzzed with the usual hustle, but at the ticket counter, all was eerily quiet. Denise and Carmen stood side by side, checking in passengers, their minds thick with unspoken thoughts about last night's events.

"Good morning, ladies," Timothy chirped as he approached, sporting a bright smile.

"Good morning, Timothy," Carmen replied cheerfully.

But Denise, her expression icy, turned away.

"Next in line, please," she snapped, not in the mood for pleasantries. Timothy's smile faltered a fraction, and he adjusted his Captain's hat nervously.

"You have a great day, Denise," he said, attempting to maintain his friendly demeanor as he moved on. After he walked away, Carmen leaned closer to Denise.

"Was that really necessary? You could have been nicer to Timothy." Denise ignored her, her focus already shifting to the next passenger. Abruptly, she blurted,

"I need a break," Denise gasped, her voice trembling with a mix of emotions. She bolted out of the ticket area, each step feeling like a ton of bricks as she made her way to the breakroom, desperate for somewhere to breathe. Once she was inside, she hit the cold floor hard, her sobs spilling out, each one a raw sign of her struggle.

Max's denial? That hit her like a punch in the gut,

sending Denise spiraling into a dark cloud of pain. She hugged her knees and wept in the break room. Carmen, stationed at the ticket counter, couldn't ignore the heart-wrenching sounds cutting through the usual hustle and bustle. Without thinking twice, she swung into action, her instincts kicking in.

"Herself Airlines Supervisor needed at the ticket counter, like, now!" Carmen shouted, urgency coursing through her voice.

The Supervisor rushed in, worry painted all over her face, "Carmen, what's going on?"

"It's Denise. She's falling apart. I've got to help her!" Carmen explained, urgency dripping from her words, knowing they had to act fast.

"Go. I'll cover the counter," the Supervisor said, waving her on. Carmen hurried into the breakroom, finding Denise curled in a ball, rocking back and forth.

"Denise, I'm here," she said softly, kneeling beside her friend.

"Why is Max denying his baby?" Denise's voice trembled as she wiped her nose with the back of her hand, tears staining her cheeks. Carmen handed her a tissue, concern flooding her heart.

"Wait a minute. Let's think about this."

"There's nothing to think about! I have to make Max remember that night we were together!" Denise insisted, frustration bubbling to the surface.

"Okay," Carmen replied carefully. "I think that's a good idea. Would you like me to call him and arrange a time for the two of you to meet at my house? Neutral ground."

"Can you? Would you?" Denise asked, her eyes wide with hope.

"Yes," Carmen affirmed. "It's settled. Now, get up off this cold floor. Take a break. I'll go back to the counter. Lord help us all." Taking a deep breath, Carmen returned to her duties. She glanced over at the Supervisor; she could see the concern still lingering in her eyes.

"How is she?" the Supervisor inquired.

"She's doing better," Carmen assured her.

"Good. I can't afford to lose another agent," the Supervisor replied, her tone stern.

Just then, Denise emerged from the breakroom, wrapping her arms tightly around Carmen. "Thank you," Denise whispered, her voice still shaky.

"I love you, Denise," Carmen said, their bond palpable in that moment. Together, they completed their shift, the weight of the unresolved tension lingering in the air.

Carmen dialed Max's number, her heart pounding.

"Hello?"

"Max, this is Carmen," she said, trying to keep her voice steady. "I need to ask you something. Are you willing to meet with Denise at my house? She wants to remind you of that night you two were together."

"Carmen, you don't know how crazy that sounds to me. The problem is, we were never together."

"I believe you, but Denise is adamant about it," Carmen insisted. After another beat of silence, Max finally spoke with determination.

"Fine. I'll meet with Denise at your home, and I'm bringing Latoya."

"Great. Today is Monday—how about next Monday?" Carmen suggested, feeling a mix of relief and tension.

"Okay. I'll clear this matter up, for the last time," he replied before they hung up.

# Chapter 10

On a tense Monday afternoon, the air in Carmen's kitchen buzzed with tension, wrapping around the four of them like a tight coil. Max sat next to Latoya, his fingers drumming an irregular beat against the table, a nervous energy pulsing through him. He swayed slightly, his body instinctively seeking solace in the rhythm of the moment.

Latoya, with her hair drawn back in a sleek ponytail, sat resolute. Her eyes flicked between Max and the table, every ounce of her focus directed at him, ready to challenge whatever came next. Across from them, Denise leaned forward, her gaze piercing into Max, tracking the tiny twitches of his face as if they held the secrets to a puzzle only she could solve.

Carmen sensed the weight enveloping them, thick and suffocating. With a swift intake of breath, she shattered the silence like glass breaking underfoot.

"Denise, you wanna take the lead?" Her voice was steady, a stark contrast to the charged atmosphere, slicing through the tension with the precision of a knife. Denise's heart raced, a drumbeat loud in her ears as she nodded. She inhaled deeply, drawing on the remnants of camaraderie as memories cascaded over her.

"Max, remember that dance floor at your annual Pilot Holiday party?" she asked, a smile tugging at the corners of her lips as warm nostalgia washed over her, momentarily lifting the heaviness in the room. "You were sweaty, tipsy, doing the 'Lindy Hop' to the sound of jazz music." Max straightened a little, his mind swirling with recollections of the lively event.

"Yeah, I remember that party," he confirmed, the memories flooding back.

With a touch of mischief, Denise added, "I walked in wearing a blond wig, five-inch stilettos, and a fiery red dress that barely covered half my thighs."

Max's posture shifted; he folded his arms defensively across his chest. Denise continued, her tone sliding into something more somber.

"We had a meaningless conversation as the day slipped into night, and then night turned into morning."

Carmen, feeling the crackling energy in the room, reached out and clasped Denise's hand in a gesture of support. Max slowly relaxed his defenses, placing his hands on the table.

With a softening voice, Denise dropped a weighty revelation.

"We woke up in your penthouse suite, and you said, without even looking at me, 'I had a great time; you can see yourself out.'"

Silence fell over the table like a heavy blanket, and Max pressed his lips together, the gravity of her words settling in. He blinked, disbelief washing over him.

"Wait—that was you?" he managed to say, realization dawning like a slow sunrise. Latoya's eyes widened, her disbelief palpable.

"So, it's true?" she asked, her voice nearly a whisper, mirroring the shock enveloping the room. Max shook his head slowly, struggling to piece together his fragmented memories.

"Honestly, I don't remember much from that night, but I do recall telling someone I had a wonderful time before they left." Latoya slumped back against her chair, her head dropping into her hands.

"I can't believe this," she murmured, disappointment weaving through her words like a shadow. In a moment of desperation, Max reached for her hands.

"I swear to you, Latoya, I didn't know. I promise," he pleaded, his voice tinged with urgency. Denise, watching him closely, narrowed her eyes.

"What do you have to say to me?" she demanded, her voice trembling with an unsettling blend of hurt and anger. Carmen, sensing the escalating tension, intervened.

"Wait, everyone, take a deep breath," she urged, trying to restore some semblance of calm to the storm brewing around them. Max turned back to Denise, his tone shifting

from defensive to sincere. "Excuse me, Denise, I'm speaking to my wife," he asserted, determination lacing his voice.

Denise's voice trembled as she faced him. "I feel so sad and hurt right now. It's like my heart has been shattered, and I can't shake this heavy sense of loneliness," she confessed, her emotions spilling over.

"I wish you could understand the pain I'm in, the disrespect and shame weighing down on me. I need you to feel guilty about what you've done."

"But how can I care about something I had no idea about?" he shot back, frustration creeping into his tone. Carmen raised her voice, rising above the chaos enveloping them.

"Wait a minute, you two! Stop yelling; this isn't how we should handle this," she said, trying to steer them back from the edge. Latoya, her cheeks flushed and glistening with sweat, abruptly stood up, desperation flashing in her eyes.

"I need fresh air," she declared, stumbling toward the front door, her breath coming quicker. Max sprang into action, rushing after her as the door swung open behind her.  Left behind, Denise sought solace in a Coke from the refrigerator, the cool metal offering a brief respite from the storm brewing in her heart. She sank into a chair at the table across from Carmen, who remained steadfastly trying to untangle the emotional mess that had erupted in her kitchen. Carmen prompted Denise gently.

"Okay, Denise, talk to me." She inched closer, sensing the storm brewing within her friend. "If what you're saying is true, then it's possible that Max is your baby's father. But he just found out; he had no way of knowing about your pregnancy."

Denise turned away, her gaze lost somewhere beyond the window. The weight of her sorrow was palpable, a heavy cloud that lingered in the air. "Well, he knows now," she replied, her voice thick with bitterness. Carmen pressed on, trying to navigate the tangled web of emotions.

"Yes, he does. But now what? Should he divorce Latoya and marry you?"

"No! I'm not saying that!" Denise snapped, frustration bubbling to the surface like a boiling pot about to overflow.

"It sure sounds like it," Carmen shot back, an edge of concern creeping into her tone. "Denise, listen to me. Max is married to Latoya, and that's not going to change." In that moment, it was as if Carmen's words fell into a void, and Denise was lost in her own chaotic thoughts.

Besides, Carmen continued, "Max prayed for a second chance with Latoya." The hope behind her words was clear, but it only worsened Denise's pain.

"That's not what happened," Denise insisted, her voice rising with indignation, every syllable laced with pain.

"I helped Max reunite with Latoya. I did that." The weight of her confession hung between them, a painful reminder of their intertwined lives. Carmen felt a mix of concern and disbelief wash over her, stunned by the profound betrayal that had unfolded.

"Oh wow, Denise, are you really serious right now?" Carmen chuckled, a playful tone in her voice. "I mean, I was just sitting here with my popcorn, waiting for the moment you'd realize what you did! You pretended to play matchmaker for those two, but come on, did you honestly think they'd end up married like this? And here we are! It's like we're in some romantic comedy and you're the unexpected plot twist. What's next, a sequel?"

Denise shifted her focus back to the window, pulling the curtains aside with a longing gaze as if searching for Max and Latoya outside. "You're right—I didn't think Latoya would take Max back," she admitted, resignation creeping into her voice. "And yes, I thought maybe Max, and I would have a chance together." Carmen's expression softened, sympathy washing over her.

I'm sorry for you, Denise. Things didn't turn out the way you wanted. But don't you think it's time to let bygones be bygones?" Denise turned sharply, her eyes blazing with emotion.

"I expect you to say that because you've never been in love. Perfect, Carmen." Carmen's heart ached at Denise's words.

"Far from perfect over here. Denise, I take offense to that! I get your pain, I really do. You've been through so much, and it's perfectly normal to feel a bit broken. But to say I've never been in love? Oh, honey, I've done the love tango! I've been in love, out of love, and worst of all, love was snatched from me when I was just a teenager, barely able to download a ringtone!

I got pregnant at sixteen, and my parents put my baby boy up for adoption. I've been dreaming of finding him, telling him how much I love him, and that, unfortunately, I didn't exactly have a 'Mom of the Year' award to wave around." Carmen is not able to hold back tears.

"Denise, I know all about that smile you put on to hide the hurt, but listen, some battles aren't meant to be fought alone. When you feel like you've done all you can, that's when peace decides to throw a party. You have to let go and let God handle the rest," Carmen said, her words infused with the wisdom of her experience.

"God sees every tear and every burden we carry. However, you need to stop blaming Max and yourself for what happened. Healing is all about surrendering the past, and girl, you deserve a good night's sleep!" Carmen chuckled lightly, trying to lighten the mood.

"Lift your hands, take a deep breath, and let it be. Life might feel like chaos right now, but I promise, God doesn't pull the rug out from under you—he's more of a 'let's redecorate' kind of guy. Trust me, it can work out even if you feel like you're living in a romantic comedy gone wrong!" Carmen paused, her expression earnest as she looked at Denise. She understood well the pain of wearing a smile to mask the hurt.

"I know all about it," she began softly. "But some battles aren't meant to be fought alone. When you feel like you've done all you can, that's when peace decides to throw a party. You have to let go and let God handle the rest."

Carmen's love for both Denise and Latoya surged within her, fueling a quiet strength that urged Denise to see the bigger picture.

"This situation needs to change. Denise, you have to remember what's truly at stake."

But Denise crossed her arms defiantly, hurt and frustrated, the hurt and frustration bubbling to the surface.

"Let me take a guess—Max and Latoya's feelings, right?"

"No—well, yes, but you also need to think about your baby. You must consider what's best for your unborn child."

Anger flared in Denise, and a mix of emotions churned inside her.

"Max, Latoya, and the baby. What about me, what about my feelings? Cries, Denise."

Carmen felt the weight of Denise's struggle, the urgency rising like a tide. Denise's voice trembled, tangled in anger, fear, and a profound sense of loss. She felt torn between her own emotions and the overwhelming responsibility for her unborn child.

"Denise, it's not just about you. It's about the life you're bringing into this world. Your feelings matter, but you've got to think about your baby's future."

The tension between them thickened, yet in that moment, their eyes locked, and both women sensed the intertwining weight of love, loss, and hope that filled the room. Change waited just around the corner. The road ahead was uncertain, yet it might lead to healing, redemption, and a love stronger than the tangled mess they found themselves in.

Then, the front door swung open, and Max and Latoya stepped into the house, taking their seats beside Denise at the table.

Momentarily silenced by their arrival, Denise shifted her attention. Carmen sat in the chair opposite her. Max reached out and gently squeezed Denise's hand.

"Denise, I'm sorry for lashing out earlier; that was no way to talk to you," Max explained. "I should have been more sensitive to your feelings. I am sorry."

Denise's eyebrows lowered as sadness fought with her lingering anger.

"I'm sorry too!" cried Denise. "I should have told you sooner about the baby." Stealing a glance at Latoya. "Latoya, I'm sorry for disrupting your wedding reception celebration, please forgive me," she whispered.

Max and Latoya responded in unison.

"We Forgive you."

Denise lifted her gaze, her tone growing stronger.

"I'm sorry for everything. I promise you both won't have to worry about me interfering in your lives anymore."

"Thank you, Denise."

"And Carmen, please forgive me for the harsh words I said to you."

With her head bowed and her hands pressed together in a gesture of sincerity. Carmen glanced up, gratitude illuminating in her eyes.

"Thank you, God. Denise, I will forgive you, but only on one condition."

"Condition? What is that?" Denise asked, confused.

"Come with me to church on Sunday. We're having our annual Bring a Friend to church day, and I would love for you to be my guest." "Church?" Denise echoed, hesitating at first.

But Carmen stood, smiling, beaming at her friend. "Sure, why not? I'll come."

Good. I will pick you up on Sunday at 10 a.m." Carmen said, her excitement visible as Max, Latoya, and Denise settled in for a pizza dinner at the table.

The aroma of the freshly baked pizza wafted through the air, mixing with their laughter and the warmth of shared moments. The atmosphere lightened, each chuckle and shared glance weaving a thread of connection that promised healing and hope.

* * *

In the warm embrace of a church service, Denise settled into the front pew next to Carmen, letting the choir's melodious harmonies wash over her. The air was filled with a sense of peace, a moment of solace amidst life's chaos. But that tranquility was disrupted when the heavy door creaked open.

Her heart quickened as she spotted Timothy entering. As his gaze found hers, she felt an unmistakable connection, a mix of hope and anxiety churning within her as he approached, clutching a plain cream-colored envelope.

Denise's smile flickered, dimming as she registered the serious expression etched on his face. A knot formed in her stomach, and she instinctively tensed.

"Timothy. I didn't know you were coming," she said, her voice bright but tinged with worry, hoping to bridge the gap between them.

"We need to talk," he stated, standing over her, his shadow looming large, a physical representation of the weight of their conversation. Concern swelled inside her.

"Is everything okay? You look…" She struggled to finish her thought, hoping to offer him some comfort amid his obvious distress.

"…Is it? Everything okay? Tell me, Denise," he pressed, his voice laced with urgency and vulnerability, and it pierced through her heart.

Feeling the weight of the other congregants' gazes, Denise glanced around nervously.

"Timothy, can we not do this here?" she pleaded, her spirit weighed down by the fear of judgment.

"Why not? It's God's house. It's perfect," he replied, pushing the envelope across her Bible, stopping just short of her trembling hands. I need to know if the baby's mine," he said, his words hitting her like a physical blow, raw and unfiltered. Denise felt a mix of dread and sorrow washing over her.

"I already told you, it's not your baby, but… whatever," she managed, trying to mask her anxiety with indifference, even though doubts gnawed at her insides. Timothy let out a bitter scoff, a humorless laugh that cut through the air.

"Whatever. That's one way to put it. 'Deceitful' is another, open it, his voice low but filled with an emotion she couldn't ignore.

Denise felt a swirling tempest of emotions. With shaking hands, she reluctantly picked up the envelope, its texture feeling both foreign and heavy in her grasp.

"What is this?" she asked, her voice barely more than a whisper, reflecting her overwhelming uncertainty.

"It's the first step toward the truth. We need to resolve this, once and for all," Timothy said, his tone steady yet laced with desperation. As Denise tore open the flap, she pulled out the form, her heart racing as she read the header. It felt as if the air had been sucked out of her lungs. It was a paternity test form, and her world turned upside down in that instant.

"You can't be serious," she whispered, the reality of the situation crashing over her like a wave.

"I'm serious. You have a choice: we can handle this quietly, or we can involve lawyers. It's your decision." He took a seat directly behind her, his gaze fixed on her with a mix of frustration and a yearning for clarity.

For a moment, Denise was immobilized, the form trembling in her grasp as she absorbed the tumult of emotions swirling around them. The choir's beautiful music faded into the background as her heart raced with fear and confusion. Carmen, sitting nearby, sensed the tension and shot a worried glance at Denise's way, silently offering support.

In that moment of vulnerability, Denise felt the weight of the world on her shoulders. Life had thrust her into a challenging situation, but she understood that even in the darkest moments, there lay an opportunity for growth and healing. She realized that confronting the truth, though daunting, was an act of courage and strength.

As she gathered her thoughts, a flicker of determination ignited within her. Love and honesty were essential, and perhaps, just perhaps, this was the moment they could reclaim their narrative.

With empathy filling her heart, she reminded herself that they were both seeking understanding, and she knew she had to respond to Timothy, not just with words, but with the vulnerability that could bring them closer to a resolution.

As the preacher spoke about forgiveness, Denise leaned in, really listening to what he had to say.

"We've got to learn to forgive," the preacher emphasized. "It's the only way to find joy, peace, and a path forward."

Carmen could see something shift in Denise. Suddenly, she stood up, her heart pounding, and walked to the altar.

"I forgive, and I want forgiveness," her voice shaky but full of emotion. The preacher smiled and reached out his hand.

"Hallelujah! What's your name?"

"I'm Denise Morgan, and I want to know Jesus," her voice gaining strength.

"Denise Morgan confesses that she wants to know Jesus," the preacher announced to the congregation.

Carmen felt a swell of pride as she stepped closer to Denise and wrapped her arm around her shoulders.

"Repeat after me," the preacher instructed. "Dear Lord Jesus, I know I am a sinner and ask for your forgiveness."

Denise followed along, her heart racing with every word.

"Do you believe what you just prayed?" he asked, his eyes locked on hers.

"Yes, I do!" she affirmed passionately.

"Then, according to the Bible, you are saved!" he proclaimed, and Denise felt a wave of relief flood over her.

"Thank you, Jesus! Thank you, Jesus!" she exclaimed, her heart overflowing with gratitude. The congregation stood up, welcoming Denise into her new life. Timothy stepped in for a warm hug, while Carmen raised her hands in thanks, tears of joy streaming down her cheeks.

"Thank you, Jesus, for forgiving Denise's sins and saving her soul," she whispered, her heart so full.

Later, as Carmen drove through the lively city streets, she couldn't help but smile, celebrating Denise's big decision and feeling a joyful excitement bubbling inside her.

* * *

Two months have passed since Denise joined the church. Carmen and Latoya navigated the long lines, while Denise stood in the corner, looking strained as her pregnancy neared its end. Carmen noticed Denise had a frown; concern etched on her face.

"Denise, I can't believe you're still working after your doctor recommended bed rest."

Denise managed to make a tired smile.

"This is my last week working; then I'll follow the doctor's orders," she replied, trying to sound more upbeat than she felt.

Carmen said firmly, "That's good because you really don't look well. You look like the baby is ready to come."

Denise shook her head, dismissing the concern, "Nah, I have two more weeks before my bundle of joy arrives."

Latoya, who was busy attending to customers, announced, "Ladies, I'm going to break." She turned and noticed Denise bent over, her eyes wide with alarm.

"Denise, are you okay?" Latoya rushed over, her voice tinged with worry.

"No, no," Denise gasped, then suddenly collapsed forward against the ticket counter.

Panic flooded Carmen as she yelled, "Supervisor! Please, call an ambulance now!" Her heart was pounding.

Denise's voice trembled with fear, "I can't feel my legs."

In a swift moment, a gush of pale-yellow liquid flowed down Denise's legs, and the reality of the situation hit them like a cold wave.

"Breathe, Denise, breathe," Latoya urged, her voice steady despite the chaos.

"I'm having my baby. Can somebody call Max?"

Denise cried out in a mixture of fear and desperation, and within moments, two paramedics rushed through the airport entrance. The male paramedic, appearing to be in his thirties, and his younger partner quickly rolled Denise onto a gurney and gingerly placed her in the waiting ambulance. Latoya climbed in beside her, gripping. Denise's hands tightly.

"I'm here with you, Denise," she said, her tone reassuring.

"Thank you, Latoya. Did you call Max?" Denise gasped, sweat beading on her forehead. "Not yet," Latoya replied, her focus clear on her friend's well-being.

Carmen didn't waste any time. She pulled her phone from her pocket and dialed Max's number.

"Max, Denise is in labor," she said, urgency lacing her voice.

"What? Labor? Where is she?" Max responded, clearly concerned.

"She's been taken to Baptist Medical Center," Carmen informed him.

"I'm on my way," Max replied before Carmen hung up and quickly turned her attention to Timothy.

"Timothy, Denise is in labor," she said breathlessly.

"I'm on my way, —which hospital?" his voice steady, though concern lingered beneath.

"Baptist Medical Center."

"Okay, I'll call Max."

"I already called him," feeling the weight of the situation settling around them. The ambulance sped down the highway, the driver weaving in and out of traffic. Latoya held Denise's hand tightly, her thoughts racing about Denise's desperate calls for Max.

"Aughhh, it hurts. It hurts," Denise groaned, her face contorted in pain. Latoya glanced at the driver, urgency in her voice.

"Can you drive any faster?"

"I'm afraid there's an accident ahead," as he slowed down to navigate the congestion.

Denise moaned softly, anxiety seeping into her voice.

"An accident! I need to get to the hospital. My baby is coming."

"No! No! The baby can't come now," Latoya insisted, trying to regain control of the situation.   The paramedic in the back of the ambulance donned a pair of gloves, preparing for what lay ahead.

"Denise, I'm going to check your dilation," he announced, his tone steady. "You're ten centimeters dilated. You're ready to give birth."

"What does that mean?" fear creeping into her voice.

"It means the baby is coming," the paramedic confirmed. Then he turned back to Denise. "The baby won't wait. Listen to me, I will help you deliver."

"No! Now, please, take me to the hospital! Aughhh! Call Max!" Denise cried, her voice filling the cramped space. Latoya shifted, positioning herself next to Denise, her expression resolute. The paramedic maintained his calm demeanor.

"Denise, there's no time. The baby is in position.

I will count to ten, and then you need to push." "Okay," Denise gasped.

"Here we go. Ten, push!" the paramedic urged.

"Aughhh! Aughhh!" Denise cried out, straining as he guided her through the process.

"You're doing great, Denise. One more time, I will count to ten again." His voice remained steady and encouraging. Denise screamed again, her body working hard as the sound of a baby crying pierced through the tension in the ambulance.

"You did it! It's a baby boy!" the paramedic announced triumphantly.

"Denise, you're a mother. He is beautiful!" Latoya exclaimed, tears of joy welling in her eyes.

"Give him to me," Denise pleaded.

Meantime, at the hospital, Max stood anxiously by the emergency door, nervously glancing at Timothy.

"Do you think Denise has picked a name for the baby?" he asked, concern etched on his face.

Timothy replied quietly, "I heard her say it's Timothy Jr."

Carmen, nearby, raised an eyebrow. "Did you say something, Timothy?"

"Oh, no," Timothy said quickly, avoiding her gaze. "Just thinking out loud."

Max sighed and stepped outside for a moment of solitude. He looked up at the sky, whispering a prayer for strength. Just then, the sound of sirens interrupted his thoughts as the ambulance pulled up. Latoya emerged from the ambulance, and Max felt a rush of relief as he saw her. A young nurse approached Denise with urgency.

"Are you Denise Morgan?" she asked.

"I am," Denise replied, her voice a mix of hope and fear.

The nurse explained, "I have orders for a mandatory paternity test." Denise hesitated but ultimately handed her baby over, her worry evident in her eyes.

"Please do it quickly and bring my baby back to me," she urged.

"Of course. By the way, have you chosen a name for your baby?" the nurse inquired. Denise smiled slightly, though still anxious.

"Yes, Timothy Maximus Morgan," she said, pride tinging her voice.

As the nurse took Timothy Maximus away, Carmen and Timothy exchanged glances, uncertainty in the air. All the while, Max wrapped his arms around Latoya, sensing her joy.

"He's beautiful," she whispered, tears brimming in her eyes.

"Yes, he is," Max responded, relieved. "Now that our part is done, are you ready for our official honeymoon?"

Latoya chuckled lightly, "In all the excitement, I almost forgot!" Max's heart lifted as he took her hand, and they ventured out of the hospital, eager for their new chapter.

In the hospital parking lot, Max dug through his bag and pulled out two airline tickets.

"I hope you don't mind, but I packed for our trip to Hawaii. Here are the tickets," he said, his excitement noticeable. Latoya's eyes sparkled as she took the tickets.

"Let's go!" Once in the car, Latoya smiled brightly.

"I'm a stepmom to a wonderful baby boy! Max, I love you, and I've forgiven your past. I want us to move forward together. If the baby is yours, he'll be our son because family is what matters most." She gently wiped the tears from Max's face, sealing their promise for the future.

At the airport, while waiting to board their flight, Latoya spotted Timothy in a corner engaged in a discussion with a woman she didn't recognize.

"What's he doing here? Who is she?" Latoya thought uneasily as they approached the gate. Then they presented their boarding passes to the gate agent and boarded the plane; the weight of the day settled on them.

Max leaned back in his seat, breathing deeply as the aircraft was in the air, engines roaring, and he felt a rush of excitement.

The cabin lights flickered, casting an eerie glow as the plane climbed through the thick, billowing clouds. Amid the mechanical hum, a tense energy built among the passengers. Latoya's grip tightened on Max's hand, the excitement that once sparkled in their eyes now replaced by a growing sense of dread.

Suddenly, Max's phone buzzed violently in his pocket, a jarring sound amid the anxious silence. He hesitated, his heart pounding as he caught

Latoya's gaze, a mixture of yearning and fear, was reflected in his eyes. She leaned forward, breath held, a silent plea for him to check his phone.

With hesitant fingers, he retrieved the phone. His heartbeat quickened as he saw the lab's email, its subject line striking him like a lightning bolt—

"Paternity Test Results."

Latoya instinctively drew closer, her eyes wide, searching his face for clues.

"It's time," she whispered, her voice barely cutting through the roar of engines. Max's breath hitched as he opened the email, the brightly lit screen illuminating the storm brewing inside him. Words blurred as he scanned the results, anxiety threading through him like a tightening noose.

Latoya's hand shook gently in his, her anxious anticipation visible. Just as he parted his lips to utter the truth that could fracture their lives, the plane bucked violently, sending him reeling.

Time slowed as the phone slipped from his grasp, tumbling through the air. He watched in horror as the screen illuminated the chilling words before the device fell to the floor:

'We are unable to determine—'

The plane lurched again, spiraling into turbulence, and Max felt a wave of dread wash over him as the light flickered out, plunging them into an abyss.

In that fleeting moment, the chaos of the world outside mirrored the tempest brewing inside them. Latoya's eyes held his with a haunting intensity, a silent question swirling between them, heavy as the clouds that enveloped them:

*Who was the father?*

# ACKNOWLEDGEMENT

I am writing to express my heartfelt gratitude to the remarkable professors and dedicated peer reviewers at Liberty University. Their teachings and unwavering support have laid a solid foundation for my novella, Emotional Entanglement: Forever. Divorced from Eternity, which is the first installment in my trilogy. Their insights have not only shaped this work but have also ignited a passion within me to pursue my storytelling.

I am deeply thankful for my family, whose love and encouragement have been a guiding light throughout this journey. A special acknowledgment goes to my husband, Minister Gerald. Your steadfast belief in me has been a wellspring of strength, reminding me that with faith and perseverance, anything is possible.

To my oldest son and devoted reader, Bruce Mckinnies II, your thoughtful feedback has been nothing short of transformational. Your insights continually inspire me to elevate the quality of my writing and push the boundaries of my creativity. I must also extend my gratitude to my beloved sister, Gloria Ann Badall. Your wise reminders, especially the verse "The eye is the lamp of the body. If your eyes are healthy, your whole body will be full of light" (Matt. 6:22 NIV), serves as a constant source of inspiration. Your guidance, combined with my personal faith, has been essential in helping me stay true to my vision and maintain my integrity throughout this process. Together, all of you have contributed to a journey that is not just about writing but about the pursuit of light, love, and transformative storytelling. Thank you for being part of my path.

I will stand at my watch and station myself on the

ramparts; I will look to see what he will say to me, and

what answer am I to give to this complaint?

Then the Lord replied: "Write down the revelation

and make it plain on tablets

so that a herald may run with it. For the revelation

awaits an appointed time; It speaks of the end and will

not prove false. Though it lingers, please wait for it; It

will certainly come and will not be delayed

"See, the enemy is puffed up;

His desires are not upright, but the righteous person

will live by his faithfulness—"

(Habakkuk 2:1-3)

# ABOUT THE AUTHOR

Ron's Photography

CYNTHIA EPHRON JEFFRESS is an inspirational fiction writer, debuting her novella, Emotional Entanglement: Forever Divorced from Eternity, the first in a poignant trilogy. Her ability to entertain and inspire others is evident on every page of this romance drama, which explores love and faith, reflecting on trusting in God's will and the transformative power of second chances. With an MFA in Creative Writing from Liberty University, Cynthia infuses her work with her faith and personal experiences. Currently living in Scottsburg, Virginia, she draws inspiration from her everyday life.

* * *

Visit her online at herselfpublishingbooks.com